THE SHADOW'S VOICE

DAVID GREENE

The Elliot Blake Novels
BOOK TWO

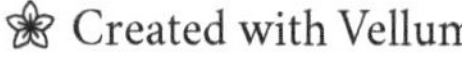 Created with Vellum

PREFACE

The Shadow's Voice is the second novel in the Elliot Blake series. Unlike the first novel, *The Winkler Case*, which echoed the noir style of *Double Indemnity*, the style of *The Shadow's Voice* is mostly playful.

The plot incorporates a mystery involving the actors of a fictional 1948 radio drama. But the novel is mainly about relationships: the relationship between Elliot and Vito, and the friendships that took shape within a world hidden from the rest of society.

Gay life in 1948 was lived in secret. To protect that secret, gay people had to master intimation, talk in code, and do whatever they could to maintain plausible deniability. It is this secretiveness that drives the characters to desperate actions.

I've filled in some missing history. But I've also paid close attention to the historical record. I researched the documented history of LGBT life in the military during World War II and in Chicago after the war. What I learned was fascinating and moving.

Let this story be an ode to and a remembrance of the lives, loves and culture that the larger world tried (but failed!) to blot out. Let this story be *The Shadow's Voice*.

1

——————

Just after ten o'clock on a Saturday morning I walked past a display window at Marshall Fields' men's store, where a short man in a purple smock was arranging a suit on a mannequin. As I stopped to look, the window dresser turned to have a look at me. The suit was a double-breasted, flannel number in baby blue, which happened to be the same color as my eyes, which meant, as far as I was concerned, I was just the baby for it. I needed a new outfit to go with my new job. Due to no fault of my own, I'd been promoted.

I tipped my hat to the dresser, walked into the store, made my way to the suit department, sized up the sales clerks, and settled on a fussy-looking, gray-haired man whose name tag identified him as 'Mr. Geiger.' Geiger was behind the cufflink display case, which was two counters over from the suit counter.

But his eyes said 'come hither,' so I went thither and told him what I wanted.

Geiger, who was nattily dressed in a gray pin-striped getup, fluttered his hand up to his neck and said, "Kiddo, I know just the one you mean. Hang on a minute." He ducked into the backroom. A moment later he came out with the suit, laid the pants on the counter, then held up the coat behind me. I slipped on the coat while he stood by with pins in his mouth ready to make adjustments, but he didn't need to. That double-breasted jacket fit me like a second skin.

Next I tried on the pants. Geiger ran a tape measure up and down my legs. Then he ran it up and down my legs one more time just to be sure. After he pinned the cuffs, I stepped in front of the three-way mirror. I turned so I could see what the pants did for me from behind. Judging from Geiger's expression, they did exactly what I wanted.

Next I roamed around the men's department while Geiger tagged along. I spotted a dark navy shirt. I picked up the shirt and handed it to Geiger, who shook his head and grimaced. After that I found a white linen tie. When I handed the tie to Geiger, he screwed up his forehead as if the sight of it made his eyes hurt. At my final stop, I picked out a white linen breast-pocket handkerchief that had a pre-folded crease so crisp it would have been impossible to blow my nose in it. This time, Geiger merely shrugged.

Geiger carried my array of accessories back to the

counter. As he folded and wrapped the shirt, he sighed and made a clucking sound. He did the same thing for the tie. When he was done he ran his hand up to his neck again and said, "You're killing me with this shirt and tie."

I told him, "Yeah? Well, that's because it's a killer combo."

Geiger shrugged. "If you say so, kiddo."

My snappy outfit might have been a little too snappy for Geiger, but it was way too snappy for Amalgamated Home and Life where I worked. I didn't care. The look was classy. It was confident. It was just what I wanted.

At eight o'clock on Monday morning I walked through the heavy glass doors of the Fisher building on Dearborn Street to start my new job. The new job came with a new office on a higher floor, the 17th, in a corner suite with windows on both sides and a bird's-eye view of the elevated train on Van Buren Street. When I got to my office, I stepped inside, closed the door, and went straight to the window to take in how far up in the world I'd come. A week earlier my office had been down on the 16th floor—down with the sales agents.

I turned from the window and took a seat in the leather swivel chair behind the desk. Unfortunately, the chair fit me about as well as a bathtub fits a baby.

The man who'd previously used the chair was larger. His dark walnut desk was roughly the size of a platform built to hold an elephant. Everything in my new office was big compared to what I'd had back on the 16th floor. The chair and the desk had belonged to my recently deceased predecessor, Martin Zimmerman. Martin had been both my friend and my mentor. He'd been the 'Head of Claims' at Amalgamated Home and Life. And now that job belonged to me.

Martin had tried to teach me about the claims business whenever we worked together, which happened whenever he had to investigate a claim that was made on a policy I'd sold. As we worked, Martin would expound on the insurance racket. I'd nod my head, but I was only half-listening. Now that he was gone, I wished I'd paid more attention to what he was trying to teach me.

A pile of Martin's open case files sat on a corner of the desk. I pulled cases from the stack one-by-one to study them. I was learning on the job and I had to learn fast. Two days after Martin's death, Mr. Chambers, Jr., who owned Amalgamated, had promoted me to take over as 'Head of Claims.' As far as I could tell, Junior offered me the job mainly because it was cheaper for him to promote me than to hire someone new.

On the day of my promotion, Junior came down from his office on the 18th floor. He got straight to the point. "Elliot," he said, "by now you know the insurance business backward and forward, don't you?"

Junior was a heavyset bald man with dark, bushy eyebrows. He wore a white shirt, a short black tie, and a pair of elastic brown suspenders that pulled his brown wool pants most of the way up to his chest.

He pulled the cigar from his mouth and said, "You've seen the ups and downs involved with the claims process over the years, I think."

"I know just about everything a man could know about selling insurance," I said. "Authorizing claims, on the other hand, is something else."

"But you know how the claims process works, don't you? You saw how Mr. Zimmerman went about reviewing the claims." He pointed his cigar at me. "Elliot, I could tell you a lot of gobbledygook about the claim review process, but really there are only three things you've gotta do for this job, and it's as simple as that." He counted off the three things by tapping the ash end of his cigar into the ashtray on my desk. "One, you gotta make sure the policy is paid up; two, you gotta make sure the claim is covered by the policy; and three, you gotta make sure there's no funny business involved." He raised the cigar and wagged it in the air to illustrate the vagaries of funny business. "That's the job in a nutshell. You can do those three things, can't you?" He put the cigar back in his mouth and raised his eyebrows imploringly.

"I know something about it," I said. "But I don't have the experience Mr. Zimmerman had."

"No, of course not. Nobody knew the job like Martin. But Mr. Zimmerman wasn't born with experience. He had to learn the ropes, just like anyone else. That's why I want a fellow who already knows his way around this business. After all these years I think you know what's what around here, don't you?" Mr. Chambers looked at me with hope in his eyes.

"I suppose."

"Martin always spoke well of you, Elliot. He said you were a go-getter, a square-shooter."

"Did he?"

"I can tell you this. He was set to retire in two or three years, and he figured you to take his place after he left. He wanted to begin training you for the job, but then ...." Mr. Chambers shrugged and shook his head sadly as he stubbed out his cigar in the ashtray.

"I wish there'd been time for Mr. Zimmerman to teach me," I said. "Of course, he didn't know how little time he had left."

"That's why you've got to jump into this thing head first. The company needs you."

"I don't know, Mr. Chambers. I'd better think it over."

"There'll be a raise with it, you know."

"Really?"

"Certainly. I'll raise you ten a week right away—just

for being willing to dive in. Then, if you do well with the job, why ... there's no telling."

"I could use the money," I admitted.

"Well, sure. Now look, my boy, this is a great opportunity for you. You'll move up to the 17th floor—right into Martin's old office. Not every fellow gets a chance to learn on the job and get paid for it at the same time."

"I suppose."

"So we're settled then? You'll take the job?"

"Okay." I shrugged. "If you think it's the right thing to do."

AND THAT WAS THAT. ON FRIDAY, BEFORE I LEFT WORK, I moved up to the 17th floor. My secretary, Peggy, moved all of her things to the adjoining office, which had previously belonged to Mr. Zimmerman's secretary, Margo.

Margo was no longer with the company. She'd received a large insurance settlement from Amalgamated. The settlement was big enough that she no longer needed to work. Her late father, a boxing promoter named Walt Winkler, owned a life insurance policy he'd bought from me some years ago. When Winkler died, that policy paid double—double indemnity as it was called—because the insured died in an accident on a public conveyance. Margo was the sole beneficiary on that claim. It was the last insurance claim that Mr. Zimmerman approved before he died.

In truth, Walt Winkler didn't die on a public conveyance. More importantly, his death wasn't an accident. But the real facts of the case were swept under the rug. I know because I was the one who did the sweeping. After Mr. Zimmerman died, I was the only person alive who knew what really happened to Walt Winkler. But I decided to keep quiet about it. I figured it wouldn't do anyone any good to have the truth come out.

The truth might have saved Amalgamated the cost of the death claim settlement, but it would have come at the expense of the company's reputation. I was doing Amalgamated a favor by keeping it under wraps. At least that's what I told myself. The other reason I kept quiet was because revealing the facts of the case would have disclosed information that was personal to me— information I didn't want anyone to know.

Although I was happy for Margo—happy she'd received the insurance settlement and inherited money from her father's estate—I felt rotten about how things had ended between us. I'd never really been cut out for someone like Margo. Martin Zimmerman had urged me to get a girl, and so, Margo and I had been dating. And I thought things were going great between us. But then she'd dropped me for one of her father's boxers. He was even more of a bad match for her than I was. She was better off without either one of us.

Margo had inherited her father's money, but it was someone else who'd inherited her father's house. At the time of his death, Walt Winkler had been living with another one of his boxers, a good-looking guy named Vito Vellucci. It had been a strange arrangement. Although Winkler left his money to his daughter, he left his house to Vito.

A lot of people were surprised by that. It sure as hell surprised me. I suppose Vito was the most surprised of all. Winkler, when he was alive, had taken advantage of Vito at every opportunity. When the odds were right, he'd ordered Vito to take a fall in the ring so he could cash in while betting against him. But as it turned out, Winkler must have had a soft spot in his heart for Vito, even though he'd never shown it while he was alive.

Winkler wasn't the only one with a weakness for Vito. By the time Winkler died, Vito and I had grown very close—so close that we were always in each other's company.

But I hadn't seen or spoken to Vito for weeks. The last time I'd seen him I'd been a heel. He'd been drunk. I'd been jealous. I'd let myself get worked up because I thought he'd been dating Margo behind my back. That turned out not to be true. Once I found out it wasn't Vito who'd made the move on Margo, I realized how wrong I was about him.

Vito hadn't contacted me since that night. After the way I treated him, I assumed he'd never want to see me again. But I wanted to see him. In fact, I couldn't think about anyone or anything else.

I came up with a plan. Even though I was no longer a salesman, I asked Mr. Chambers to send me out on one last sales call. Since Vito was the new owner of Winkler's house, it stood to reason that he ought to get the house insured in his own name. I already knew everything I needed to know about the house from my work on Winkler's policy. All I had to do was rewrite it in Vito's name.

When I told Junior about my plan, he said, 'Good idea. You'd better go out and see him since you already know the guy.'

That evening I picked up my newly-tailored, baby blue suit from Geiger at Fields. The next morning, I wore the suit to work. At 11:00 I left the office and took the elevated train up to the Bryn Mawr stop, then walked to Winkler's old house on Magnolia Street.

If I'd had any nerve, I'd have telephoned first. Under the circumstances, I was pretty sure Vito would've told me not to come. But I figured if he saw me in person, if he saw how sorry I was, if he saw how ashamed I was about how I'd behaved, then maybe he'd forgive me. And if he didn't, well I still wanted one last chance to see him. I had to try.

I stood in front of the door of his house straightening my new linen tie while I worked up my courage. The last time I'd come to Winkler's house to see Vito I'd been full of anticipation. This time, I was in a cold sweat. I knocked. I waited. I waited two minutes. I knocked again. After another minute, I knocked even louder. Then I craned my neck and peered into the house through the front window. There was no movement inside. I decided Vito must not be home, so I turned to leave.

And there he was, at the bottom of the steps, watching me, not saying a word, blinking his steel gray eyes. He had on a brown tweed jacket over his maroon football sweater. He held a satchel of books, which told me he'd just come home from his morning classes at the University of Chicago. Besides being a boxer, he was studying for a degree in astronomy. The strange mix of things that made him tick fascinated me. I didn't know how someone could make a living staring at the stars all night, but Vito loved staring at the stars. And now he was staring at me, wordlessly, piercing me with those cold gray eyes, the ones that made me weak in the knees.

2

"What are you doing here, Elliot?" he asked.

"I came to sell you insurance," I said.

His eyes flashed. "You've used that excuse before."

He was right. The first time I'd seen him was when I'd come to the house to sell Winkler a car insurance policy for his new car. Back then it had been Vito, not Winkler, who'd come to the door. That was how I first got to know him.

"It's not an excuse," I said. "I really do have insurance to sell you—for the house this time, now that you own it."

"That's why you're here?" He shook his head and frowned. But it was his black hair glistening in the cloudy light that drew my eyes. "Didn't it ever occur to you that I might like it better if you'd just come to see me because you wanted to see me? That's the way friends usually visit friends."

"I thought ..." I stammered. "I thought I needed a reason to see you. I didn't think you'd see me otherwise."

"So you decided to just show up at my door in that fancy blue suit and give me no choice."

"I'll leave if that's what you want."

He didn't respond at first. When he finally spoke, he stared at the ground without looking at me. "I don't know what I want." Then he glared up at me. "But one thing I don't want is insurance." He stood silently for a moment until a thin smile emerged on his lips. "I'm not afraid of risk, Elliot."

"Right." I nodded. "I should have known that about you."

"If I was, I'd never have gotten involved with *you*." He spat the word 'you.'

I stared at him, startled by his sudden tone. I didn't know what to say.

He set his satchel of books on the ground, then stood up and raked his fingers through his hair, while he glared at me. "Damn it, Elliot," he said. "What were you thinking?"

"Look, Vito," I began. "I'm sorry. OK?" I tilted my head back, as if I was speaking to the sky, because I didn't have the nerve to look at him. "I was a heel. I know I was a heel. But it's because I had everything wrong about you and Margo. When I thought you were seeing her, I was jealous." I looked straight at him to emphasize my point. "I was crazy jealous, Vito."

"Because you thought I was seeing your girlfriend?"

"Yes, but not because of her. I was jealous because of you. I thought you liked her more than you liked me. I thought you'd walked out on me."

"Walked out on you? How could I walk out on you? Think about it, Elliot. You've never once told me anything that would suggest there was a commitment on your part that I might walk out on."

I was quiet for a minute as I took that in. Then I closed my eyes. I said, "Vito, you know that's not true. You know how I feel about you."

"No, Elliot. I don't. And that's the point. You've never been able to say just how you feel about me."

"All right," I said, and I opened my eyes. "If that's what you want, I'll tell you how I feel." I looked around. "But can we go in the house? I don't want to talk about it out here on your front steps."

"Fine," he said, though he said it so softly I could barely hear him. He came up to the top of the stairs, stepped around me, unlocked the door and pushed it open. We both went inside. A moment later he flipped the light switch and the bank of spotlights came on in the living room. Nothing had changed in the room since the last time I'd been there. Walt Winkler's theatrical spotlights still lit up the same showy objects positioned around the room, including the ornate oil portrait of Winkler himself that hung on the wall.

I gestured at the painting. "Are you gonna keep that picture up there?" I went up to the painting and stood beneath it. "It's creepy to look at now that he's dead."

"Walt's portrait?" Vito shrugged. "Yeah, it stays. I'm not changing anything about this place."

"Why?"

"Because I'm selling this house and everything in it. You didn't think I'd want to live here, did you? What would I do with all this …" He swept his hand around the room. "… with all this junk of his?"

I shrugged. "You don't want any of it?"

"No. And I feel the same as you about that painting. It gives me the willies. Walt left his mark everywhere in here. The whole place is cluttered with his stuff. The sooner I can get out of here, the better."

"Where will you live?"

"In Hyde Park. In a dorm. I'll be closer to my classes. And it's cheap, especially with three guys to a room."

"You want to live in a dorm?"

"Why not? It beats living alone. I know two guys who're looking for a roommate. We already take classes together. It'll make it easier to study and share notes."

I frowned. I didn't like the idea of Vito moving, let alone the idea of him living with two other guys. "Do these friends of yours know about you?"

"What do you mean? Know about what?"

"You know."

Vito, as was his habit, stepped in front of the

spotlight that lit up the sofa. Once again his rich black hair glistened in the light. "I'm not sure what you're asking. If you're asking if they know I'm a boxer? Then yeah, they know all about it."

"That's not what I meant."

Vito plopped down on the sofa. "Look, Elliot," he said. "I don't know how to figure you. If you're talking about the way I feel about certain men—then, no, I don't talk about that with anyone who doesn't feel the same way. I don't talk about it anymore than you do. What a dumb thing to ask."

"Well, I just thought maybe they were ... I mean, I thought maybe these fellows felt the same way—like you and me, like how we feel about other guys."

Vito blinked. "Oh, I get it. You think I'm planning to move in with a couple of guys so we can all get chummy together."

"Well ..."

"Jesus, Elliot. You obviously don't understand how it works for me. I don't get hot and bothered over every guy I meet." He rubbed the top of his leg. "These two students ... they're nice, but they're squares. They're university boys. Guys who study astrophysics tend to be like that."

"Except you."

"Yeah, well. I'm not like anyone else."

That was true. He sat on the sofa, lit once again by another spotlight. His legs were spread. His hands were clenched behind his head as he leaned back on the cushion. Even through the soft contours of his sweater I could see the solid shape of his torso. And then there was his face, beneath that mop of curly black hair.

I shifted my weight on my feet as I stood before him. "But what about me, Vito? You used to get hot and bothered over me."

He nodded. "Yes. I did." Then he leaned forward, pulled his sweater off, and set it on the sofa beside him. Beneath the sweater he wore a t-shirt, plain white, very tight at the chest and biceps. He leaned back on the cushion, put his hands behind his head, and closed his eyes as if he was contemplating what I'd said. After a moment, he turned his head to face the wall. He whispered, "I still do."

"Really?" I heard my voice crack, like I was a teenage kid.

He looked back at me. His gray eyes narrowed for a moment. "As far as I can see you haven't gotten any uglier since the last time I saw you. Why would I feel any different?" He blinked and gave me a cynical smile. "Oh, you mean because you're a jerk and a heel and because you treated me worse than Winkler ever did."

"Look, I'm sorry. I was jealous. I told you. It was a misunderstanding. It was Bobolink. He told Margo he was you when he was seeing her."

"So I heard."

"And Margo told me you were her boyfriend, that you kissed her the way she wanted to be kissed—better than I ever did. So I didn't know what to think. I thought you'd been playing me for a fool."

The corners of his eyes crinkled. "I don't know which is worse," he said. "That you have so little confidence in me, or that you have so little confidence in yourself."

I nodded, a little too hard. "You're right. I don't have confidence in myself." I shrugged. "It's because I can't believe someone like you would really be interested in a guy like me."

"Why not?" He studied me with obvious puzzlement. "What's wrong with a guy like you? I mean, in your opinion."

"Well, I'm a nobody. I'm an insurance agent, which is kind of pathetic." I heard myself swallow as I spoke.

"Pathetic? Why? What's wrong with selling insurance? Is there something else you want to do?"

"No. It's not that. It's just that when I look at you I can't compare myself." I pointed at him, and waved my hand up and down. "You've got everything. You're handsome. You're strong. You're athletic. And you're smart—much smarter than I am. That's the worst of it. I don't see how I could ever be smart enough for you."

"Hmmm." Vito closed his eyes and let his head slump back into the sofa cushion. "Maybe you're right." He rubbed his forearm thoughtfully, then opened his eyes. "Maybe I should hold out for someone smarter."

"You probably should."

"But you know, Elliot, I don't have any more control

over what makes me tick than you do. I can't figure why you don't know that. The truth is, from the first time I saw you, I was knocked out. And, for a while there, I was down for the count. I couldn't get back up. Not just because of how you look—which, by the way, is pretty damn good in that blue suit. But because you were so eager to get to know me. Do you remember our date at the planetarium? You were like a puppy. Do you know how that made me feel? We had fun together. And do you remember how you held my hand after I got clobbered by Bobolink at the Chicago Stadium? I had to send Mookie out of the room because I couldn't let him see me cry."

"I remember."

"The truth is, Elliot, you're obvious. I can tell everything about you with one look. And though you try to pretend to be what you're not, you can't—not really. Your shyness, your earnestness, your vulnerability, your desire—they're written on your face in big letters, despite the facade. Hell, even now you're looking at me the way a kid looks at a candy bar he wants to unwrap."

"Well," I said. "It's no wonder I expect you to know how I feel. If you know all that, you should know how I feel about you."

"That's just it. I don't. I know you want me ... I know you want my body. But, I don't know how you feel about me. I don't know how you feel about the me inside this body."

"Oh." I blinked. "I think I get it," I said. "I don't think I did get it until just now, but now I do."

"So?"

"So you must be more of a blockhead than I am," I said. "What do you think it meant when I went with you to the planetarium and up to Yerkes observatory and when I came down to the locker room after the match at the Stadium and when I went into the woods with you on Vision hill? You think it was just because of your body?"

"I don't know, because you've never said."

"Well, let me say it now, Vito. It's you. It's you I want. It's all the things you are. Yes, that includes your body, which I have to admit makes me drunk just looking at it. But it's also because of your brains and your courage and your perseverance and how gentle you are inside all that strength you have." As I said the word 'gentle,' my voice broke and my eyes got wet. "And it's even because of how you like me. Nobody has ever liked me that way before. You talk about being down for the count. I got hit so hard by you I'm still in a daze. I want you, Vito—and nobody else. And I never thought I'd ever feel this way about anybody, 'cause I always thought I'd have to feel like this about someone like Margo. I never imagined how it would really feel. But now I'm sure of it. I love you!"

Before I finished talking, Vito was up on his feet. He had his arms around me and tugged me down onto the couch. Then, before I knew it, he pulled his t-shirt off and drew my head down to him until my face was buried in his bare chest. Every part of me was aware of the softness of his skin and of the firm muscles of his chest and of the acrid smell of his sweat. And then we just stayed that way, both of us trying not to sob, neither of us speaking. We both knew we felt like crying because we were happy. I could hardly believe my luck. It felt so good to make up with him—better than anything I'd ever experienced before. For the first time I was sure how I felt about him. And I really believed he felt the same way about me. So there we were, two grown men, a couple of lugs sitting on the sofa, not saying a word, but brother, we were in love.

3

———

Vito and I covered a lot of ground that afternoon. For one thing, I convinced him not to sell the house, at least not right away. We knew that if we wanted to spend our nights together, it would be easier to do so at his house. I couldn't sleep overnight in his college dormitory. And he couldn't sleep overnight in my apartment without the risk of my nosy landlady taking notice. Neither of us thought that was a good idea.

Vito's house on Magnolia Street was the only place where we had complete privacy. There was no one on the floor above or below who could hear us.

Vito agreed to keep the house. He also agreed to buy a six-month home insurance policy. Nothing could have pleased me more. It was as if he'd made a six-month commitment to our relationship. I promised him Amalgamated's best premium rate. How could he say no?

From that point on we were together all the time. My apartment lease was about to expire. I told my landlord I wouldn't be renewing it. I officially moved into Vito's house. It was the biggest commitment I'd ever made in my life. It seemed very sudden. Yet I had no doubt it was what I wanted.

I was glad to no longer be living alone. For the first time in my life I lived with someone I could turn to for advice about work. I knew Junior expected me to jump into my new job feet first and take off running. But the truth was, I was in over my head. I'd studied Zimmerman's notes, which were helpful, but only up to a point. The problem was that each insurance claim was different. Learning what I might have to do in one case didn't always prepare me to know what I might have to do for the next one.

During the first days in my new job I realized that most claims were easy to approve. One death claim that came in was filed on behalf of an elderly woman who died of a heart attack. She'd dropped dead at the A&P holding a basket of cantaloupes while waiting in the checkout line. I couldn't see any way that wasn't a natural death.

Then there was the car claim from a hot-rod lover who'd banged up his roadster while driving home from a party. The hot rodder had a car insurance policy with a high premium. When the salesman marked his policy as high risk, Junior knew from the get-go that insuring the guy was a gamble. Junior approved the policy, so I approved the claim. We paid out to have Mr. Hot Rodder's car fixed fair and square. Of course, Junior raised his premium even higher in anticipation of the next time he drove home from a party.

But not all the claims were so cut and dried. And those were the cases where, even though I knew I wasn't supposed to, I talked over the circumstances of the claims with Vito. I thought of it as being like a game. Vito would play the voice of doubt. He'd say, "well, what about this?" or "what about that?"—trying to cast suspicion on the merits of the claim. I had to refute his doubts, which helped me to shoot down my own. The game also helped when it came to writing up my report for Junior, since I learned to describe the pros and cons of each claim.

It wasn't long before Junior told me that since I'd learned the ins and outs of the job so quickly, he was giving me another five dollar raise. I was grateful. But Junior's confidence in me also made me anxious. I had the feeling that I was getting by mostly on luck. I also had the feeling that sooner or later my luck would run out.

Then the morning came when my secretary, Peggy, walked in and held up a thick envelope. "This just came in," she said. "It's a new death claim."

I knew Peggy had to skim over each piece of mail when she opened it so she could see if it was a claim that had to be passed on to me or if it was some other type of correspondence. I knew she'd developed a habit of eyeballing each claim form enough to know what it was all about. So I asked her, "Did you look at it?"

"Yeah, I gave it the once over," she said. "Did you happen to see the story in the paper this morning about that radio actor, Leonard Lehnert?"

"Leonard Lehnert?" I raised my eyebrows. "You mean the star of *The Shadow's Voice*? The guy who plays Percy Ballard?"

"That's the guy. According to the story in the paper, he was in a boating accident on Sunday. And today his wife sent us a death claim. Apparently he drowned."

"Leonard Lehnert has a life policy with us?"

"He does." Peggy saw a look of alarm on my face. So she added, "Hey. Don't worry. It's not a double indemnity case. The guy was on a private sailboat." Peggy tapped the envelope in her hand. "I never miss an episode of that show. I can't believe Percy Ballard is dead. Saturday night will never be the same."

"I listen to it, too." I rubbed my forehead. I knew instinctively that this claim wasn't going to be like the others. I said, "Judging by his voice on the radio, I don't think he could have been very old."

"According to the paperwork, Mr. Lehnert was 34."

"And just like that, he's dead?"

"That's what his wife says."

"Does she say what happened?"

"In so many words. She says they were out on Lake

Michigan on September 26th in a sailboat, along with another couple who had their own boat."

"So that was last Sunday, right?"

"Yes. The accident happened four days ago."

"Did she file a police report?"

"She did everything by the book. All the paperwork is in there. And as far as I can see, she's got everything tied up with a pink ribbon. That's why it's such a thick envelope." Peggy dropped the envelope on my desk, where it landed with a thud. "Good luck, Mr. Blake," she said as she headed to the door of my office. "And if you need to know anything about that radio show, just ask me."

I didn't need to ask Peggy anything about *The Shadow's Voice*. Just like Peggy, I listened to the show every week. The sponsors made a point of recommending that listeners turn out all the lights so they could listen to the show in the dark. I always got a kick out of doing that.

The show was a radio mystery on WGN at 7 o'clock on Saturdays. In it Leonard Lehnert plays private detective Percy Ballard. Every week he has to solve a new murder mystery. The gimmick is that Ballard talks with all the suspects in such a way that none of them ever knows he's a detective, because he poses as a high-society dandy who writes a gossip column called "After Dark." When he chats with people, they assume he's looking for dirt for his column. But in reality he's gathering clues to solve the murder. Since the suspects have the idea that he's nothing more than a gossip, they never realize he's putting together a case against one of them. And we never know who he's fingered until the shadow's voice speaks.

The title of the show comes from the fact that whenever Ballard figures out who's guilty, he always nabs the murderer in the dark. He's got a phonograph record of a little speech he's made. On the record he speaks in his regular voice—a voice that's so different from his gossip columnist voice that the murderer doesn't even know who's talking.

The voice on the recording always says the same thing in an eerie, deep intonation. "Good evening," the voice says. "The time has come for justice, my friend. You know what that means, don't you? When you turn on the lights you'll find there's no way out. No one can escape the shadow's voice!"

So then, the killer turns on the lights. And every week the killer lunges toward the spot where he hears the voice coming from. But the only thing in that spot is a portable record player. During the time the record is playing, Ballard moves around behind the murderer. Then he puts a gun up to the killer's back and says, "stick 'em up!"

I have to admit, I'm a fan of the show. What I especially like is that the man everyone thinks is just a snooty fop is really the hero. And I like how he takes advantage of the suspects' preconceptions to put one over on them.

The premise of the show is similar to how I see things in my own life. Of course, I'm not anything like Percy Ballard. I'm not that smart. But Percy Ballard is a lot like Vito. Whenever people see Vito in the library in his college sweater with his glasses perched on his nose while he's studying a book, they figure he's just another egghead. They have no idea what a slugger he is in reality.

I was eager to get home after work that evening to tell Vito about the new death claim. I wasn't sure if he'd know who Leonard Lehnert was, or even if he'd ever heard of *The Shadow's Voice*. Vito always studied at the school library on Saturday nights, and I always stayed home, where I listened to the show by myself. Vito didn't think much of radio shows to begin with. He said most of them were too corny for his taste.

I wondered if what happened to Leonard Lehnert would sound familiar to Vito. What happened to Lehnert was eerily similar to what had happened to Winkler. It was as if aspects of the Winkler case were happening all over again. But Vito didn't know that Winkler hadn't died accidentally. I was the only person alive who knew that Winkler had been murdered. And I hadn't made up my mind about whether or not I would ever tell Vito the truth.

4

———————

When I arrived home after work on Thursday, Vito had just come home from school and was about to go to the gym to work out with his trainer, Mookie, which he did every Thursday night. I followed him up to the bedroom. I knew he was going to change clothes and I liked to watch him when he did. That's when I told him about the Leonard Lehnert claim. And that's when he said, "I know the guy!"

"You mean you know him in person?"

Vito nodded. "It would be more accurate to say I used to know him. We went to high school together." He peeled off his maroon sweater and then his white t-shirt. I watched him, wide-eyed as a puppy. "He and I were on the wrestling team," he said.

"That's quite a coincidence." I thought for a moment. "Are you sure it's the same guy?"

Vito lifted an eyebrow. "With a name like that? How many guys with the name Leonard Lehnert could there be?"

"You're right." I nodded. "It must be him. But what are the odds that you'd know him?"

Vito shrugged. "Beats me." He walked out of the bedroom and down the hall to the bathroom. I followed him. There he took a washcloth, wet it, and wiped under his armpits.

I watched him in the bathroom mirror. "Did you know he became a big radio star?" I asked. The fluorescent tube above the bathroom mirror wasn't a flattering light. But Vito, with his flawless complexion, still managed to look good in it. "He's in a show on Saturday nights on WGN."

Vito shrugged. "It doesn't surprise me." He bent over the washbowl and splashed water on his face. Then he stood up, grabbed a towel and wiped his cheeks and forehead. "In high school, he was in the theater club. He was quite the cut-up."

"Did you ever wrestle him?"

"Once or twice." Vito walked back to the bedroom and I followed him back there. He took a clean white t-shirt from his dresser and pulled it on. "But I only wrestled him for practice. For his practice, not mine. He asked me to." Vito put on a light blue sweatshirt over his t-shirt. "Leonard wasn't a match with me," he said. "He was in a different weight class. He was thin, and I was ... bigger." Vito looked in the mirror and fussed with his hair. "He had more gumption than he had strength. I always wondered why he went out for wrestling. It didn't suit him."

"Maybe he wanted to impress his girlfriend."

"I don't know." Vito looked thoughtfully in the dresser mirror for a moment. "Did you say he was married?"

"Yes. His wife's name is Gloria. She filed the death claim."

Vito pursed his lips. "That surprises me."

"Why? Did you know her?"

"No." Vito shook his head. "I don't think so. I don't remember anyone named Gloria in high school."

I stood so Vito could see me in the mirror behind him. "Then why are you surprised?"

Vito turned around to face me. "I'm surprised because I didn't think Leonard was the marrying kind. Back in high school, I wouldn't have expected it."

"What's that supposed to mean?"

"I think you, of all people, Elliot, would have some idea what that's supposed to mean."

I sat down on the bed. "Wait. Are you saying what I think you're saying?"

A smile tugged on Vito's lips. "Yes, Elliot. I am."

"Did you and he ...?"

Vito shook his head and turned back to face the mirror. "No. There was nothing like that."

"Then what?"

"I'll just say that when Leonard Lehnert and I wrestled, his hands didn't always end up in the most natural spots—the spots where I expected them to be."

"He touched you? How?"

"Whatever he did, it was ... fleeting. He crossed the line a couple of times. The rest of the time, he was damn close to it."

"And you never said anything?"

"What could I say? We were wrestling. It's a contact sport." Vito turned to face me again.

I got up and stretched my arms around Vito's torso. I cupped my hands on his backside.

He narrowed his eyes. "What are you doing?"

"I'm trying to see where the line is."

"Why? Do you want to wrestle?"

"I might. Do you still have one of those wrestling singlets?"

"If I do, it won't fit me anymore."

"No?"

"I've gotten bigger."

I patted his backside. "In the most lovely way."

He pushed me aside. "I've got to get ready and you're making an awful distraction."

I sat back down on the bed and crossed my legs. "I'll be good," I said. But I had more questions about Leonard Lehnert. "So, apart from his wayward hands, what was he like?"

Vito folded up his sweater and placed it neatly in a

drawer in his dresser. "Like I said, he was a cut-up. He was theatrical. He was always being a ham. I'm not surprised he went into acting."

"I know him from the radio show, but I have no idea how he looked. What did he look like?"

Vito started taking off his school pants. "I haven't seen him in a decade. Don't you have a picture of him in your file?"

"There's no picture."

Vito folded his pants, set them on top of his dresser, pulled workout shorts from the bottom drawer and stepped into them, then turned around to face me. "In high school, the girls were crazy for him. He was good-looking, funny, and sweet-natured. He was skinny, but he filled out the crotch of his wrestling singlet in a noticeable way." Vito smiled and fluttered his eyes.

"What's that supposed to mean?"

"I think you know what that means, too." Vito held out his hands and looked at them. "That's the reason I had to be careful to keep my hands where they were supposed to be. That's why I was so aware of what was happening with his hands."

"OK, Vito. Now I don't know what to think. It sounds like you're trying to make me jealous."

"I'm just telling you how it was. Leonard Lehnert was a nice kid. I liked him. He made me laugh. But he hung out with the girls most of the time. So I never really got to know him."

"But you do know some things about him. And

since I'm going to have to investigate this claim, I hope you'll be willing to help me."

"I'll help you."

"The problem is, I don't know where to start. First of all, they haven't found his body. And I don't even know what Amalgamated's policy is about a situation like that."

"Too bad you can't ask your pal Zimmerman."

"I wish I could. I'll probably ask Peggy. She seems to know everything about company policy."

"You could ask Chambers."

"I know," I said. "But I don't want him to start thinking about how much I don't know."

"Then stick with Peggy."

"I also don't know how to be sure what happened to Leonard Lehnert was an accident," I said. "We had the same questions in the Winkler case. We didn't know if somebody pushed him overboard or if he wanted to end it all."

Vito stuffed two white towels into his gym bag. "I don't think Leonard could have committed suicide, Elliot, not in the circumstances you describe. I can't see how a guy who was suicidal would try to end it all by jumping into the lake while his wife and friends were watching him. Even if he couldn't swim, he'd have to know that someone would try to rescue him." Vito zipped up his bag, then turned to face me. "What exactly happened out there?" he asked.

"According to the police report, Leonard was drinking, enough to be drunk. His wife said he'd finished at least six bottles of beer when the accident occurred. According to her, he wasn't all that good at sailing to begin with, even though he owned a sailboat. She said they were getting ready to 'come about'—that's the term she used. I asked Peggy to look it up for me in the encyclopedia. It describes a maneuver that's used when a boat is tacking. Sailboats have to tack from side to side when they're sailing into the wind."

"I know about tacking," Vito said.

"Right," I said. "And when you're heading into the wind, you have to turn the bow of the boat into and through the wind so that the direction of the wind changes from one side of the sail to the other. When that happens, the boom, which holds the bottom of the sail, whips from one side of the boat to the other. Experienced sailors know how to handle that. But apparently Leonard was too drunk, and he didn't react quickly enough. The boom swung hard. It hit him before he could get out of the way. It knocked him over the side of the boat. It might have knocked him unconscious—no one knows."

Vito narrowed his eyes. "So what did his wife do? What did the other boat do? Why didn't they fish him out?"

I shrugged. "According to the report, his wife started shouting for help. And then the couple in the other boat steered over to her to see what was going on. But that's just it. It was after dusk. Nobody could see where he was. He just disappeared."

Vito cocked his head. "And they never found his body."

"Yeah. That's what doesn't seem right. He should have washed up on shore somewhere. You remember how Winkler's body floated up out by Navy Pier. That's what's supposed to happen."

"Maybe Leonard was wearing something that weighed him down."

"Like what?"

"I don't know—some kind of heavy boots, maybe."

"There's nothing about him wearing boots in the report. I think he'd have to have been wearing an anchor to stay lodged on the bottom of the lake for so long. It doesn't add up."

"I have to go," Vito said. Then he smiled at me. "Cheer up, maybe his body will turn up soon. Then you can stop worrying about whether or not he's dead and pay the claim."

"I thought you were supposed to be the voice of doubt. It seems to me that you're taking my role in this situation."

"I take whatever role is the opposite of the role you take. That's how it works."

"Oh it is, is it?"

"Yeah." Vito brushed his hand across the top of my

hair. "And you like it, don't you?" He smiled and winked at me mischievously.

I smiled, too. "Yeah. As a matter of fact, I do."

5

———

When I got to work the next morning I was in a chirpy mood. I was so chirpy I was absentmindedly whistling to myself. Peggy noticed. "What makes you so overjoyed?" she asked.

Had I been honest, I'd have told Peggy it was Vito who'd made me overjoyed. I felt like one of those dopey guys you see in the movies who walks around with his head in the clouds because some beautiful girl smiled at him. But what I said to her was, "Why not be overjoyed? It's a lovely day."

It was a nice day. But it wasn't that nice. Peggy wasn't buying it. She said, "Oh, yeah?" then gave me a cagey look and let it go at that.

My chirpiness wasn't only about Vito. I was also wound up about starting the investigation of the Lehnert case. I'd considered asking Gloria Lehnert to come up to the office to discuss her claim. But then I thought maybe I'd find out more about her if I went to her place. I also figured she'd be more relaxed at home —and maybe more talkative.

Mr. Zimmerman visited claimants at home all the time. I always thought it was a sign of his dedication. But now I realized he must have enjoyed the opportunity to take a little excursion away from the office. When Margo and I were dating, she, being Mr. Zimmerman's secretary, would sometimes tell me about his investigations. According to Margo, Zimmerman always took a cab when he went on a field trip. Then he'd write up the cost of the cab in an expense report for reimbursement. I rode the bus or took the subway whenever I went on a sales call, just like all the other salesmen. But now that I was Head of Claims I figured I'd put in an expense report, too. The thought of having an expense account added to my eager mood.

"Peggy," I said. "I'm going to take a cab to the Lehnerts' house."

"You mean a taxi cab? The kind that costs money?"

"Yeah. Why not? I'm a bigwig now. But I've never taken one before. How much should I tip the driver?"

"Oh, you could give him a quarter. Or if you're feeling generous you might give him three dimes. But be sure to get a receipt. I know from experience that Mr. Chambers is tickled pink when he sees a written receipt with the expense report."

"The Lehnerts live in Hyde Park," I said. I looked at my watch. It was 9:15. "I have an appointment with Mrs. Lehnert at ten o'clock."

"Then you better get a move on." Peggy smiled. She'd get a nice break, too, with me being away.

I went down to the curb on Dearborn Street, hailed a cab, got in and gave the driver the address in Hyde Park. In a few minutes the cab was cruising southbound on the Outer Drive. At 9:50 the driver stopped in front of the Lehnerts' address, which turned out to be a high-rise apartment building facing the lake. I gave the man a quarter plus a dime and waited patiently while he wrote out a receipt. I was too, too pleased with myself.

I took the elevator up to the seventh floor and rang the bell outside apartment 708. Almost immediately, the door opened—as if Gloria Lehnert had been standing behind the door waiting for me.

She said, "You must be Mr. Blake."

"I am. And you're Mrs. Lehnert?"

"Yes. Please come in."

I had a mental picture of what the Lehnerts' apartment might look like. But the living room surpassed my imagination. It was dominated by a row of large windows with a wall-to-wall view of Lake Michigan. I walked past all the furniture in the room and went straight to one of the windows. I couldn't resist.

Mrs. Lehnert came up next to me. "It's quite a view, isn't it?"

"It sure is." I could see waves crashing up and down the beach, but the sound didn't reach the seventh floor.

She turned and indicated a spot on a red leather sofa near the window where I could sit. "Would you like something to drink?" she asked. "I've made coffee."

"Coffee would be fine. Thanks."

She disappeared. I sat on the sofa, ran my fingers over the surface of the leather, and took in the room. The radio business must have been good. In addition to the killer view and the red leather sofa, the apartment was done up with high-quality expensive furnishings, just like Winkler had at his place: dark wood chairs with plush, embroidered cushions, a pale pink and green Oriental carpet, green glass sconces on the walls. The most distinctive feature of the room was a series of three paintings that hung on the wall facing the windows. I found myself staring at one of them. It wasn't a picture of anything I could recognize. It looked like it was supposed to be a picture of something, but whatever it was supposed to depict was broken into pieces that were scattered around, as if the painter didn't know how to put them all together the right way. And the colors, which were dirty browns and dark reds, didn't help.

When Gloria Lehnert came back in, she noticed me staring at it.

"What sort of painting is that?" I asked.

"It's a style called cubism," she said. She sat in a chair across from me.

"I never saw anything like it before," I said.

"It's modern art, Mr. Blake. Leonard was fond of cubist paintings." She gestured at the other two paintings. "We have three of them."

"Cubism," I repeated. "Are they from Cuba?"

She stifled a smile. "No. The term cubism is a reference to geometry. It's the name of an art movement in which painters break up the objects in a painting into abstract shapes so you can see them from several different angles at once."

"So what's that supposed to be a picture of?" I pointed at the painting I'd been staring at.

"That is a painting of a woman sitting in a chair."

I whistled. "Really? I'd have never guessed. But I can sort of see it now that you mention it." I stood and walked over to the painting. "So this part is the woman?" I gestured with my hand. "And this is the chair?"

"More or less," she said.

I waved my hand at the background in the painting. "What are all these other boxes and squares trailing around behind her?"

"I suppose those would be other objects in the room." She shrugged. "I don't think it matters. The artist isn't trying to be representational."

"OK," I said. "I get it. It's just like ... arty."

"No, not arty, artistic," she said. "There's a

difference." She looked at me as if I was an idiot—which at the moment I was.

"Oh. OK."

I blushed and walked back to the sofa and sat down again. On my way back, I took a good look at Gloria Lehnert. I guessed her to be in her early thirties. She was older than me, but not by much. She was what my buddy Maurice would have called 'a real looker.' Everything about her was full: full hips, full bust, full lips, full eyelashes, and a full head of curly, brunette hair. She must have kept her hairdresser busy making those curls, but the result was impressive. She was dressed like a society widow, in a black, tailor-made outfit that emphasized her figure. The somber mood of her suit was countered by the brightest red lipstick and fingernail polish I'd ever seen. A pair of emerald earrings and a jade ring added green to contrast with the red. Her eyes—deep amber and shiny—glinted from the sunlight coming through the bank of windows behind me. She looked smart. She had so much self-confidence it scared me.

"Perhaps we can get down to business, Mr. Blake. I assume you're here to talk about my insurance claim."

"Yes. I ... I'm sorry for your loss, Mrs. Lehnert." I realized I should have said that right off—as soon as I came in. That's what Zimmerman would have done.

"Frankly, I'm still trying to come to terms with it. It was completely unexpected ... obviously."

"I imagine so," I said. I tried to picture what it would be like to lose someone you loved in a flash like that.

She closed her eyes for a moment, then opened them with a forlorn look on her face. "When I wake up in the morning I have to remind myself what happened. It still feels like a dream."

"I read the report." I waved my hand from side to side in front of me. "About the boom knocking him over."

"He wasn't much of a sailor," she said. "But he should have known the sail would whip across like that. We'd come about many times before." Her shoulders sagged. "I blame myself. I shouldn't have let him drink so much."

"It's too bad he didn't know how to swim," I said. It was a lame thing to say, but I couldn't think of anything better.

"Oh, but he did know how to swim. I'm sure he knew how to swim, at least a little," she said. "But the way that sail hit him, I think it knocked him out."

I put a sympathetic look on my face. "I'm sorry to have to question you about this. As you can imagine, my company wants to know as much as possible about what happened."

"Of course."

"And to tell you the truth, I'm new to this job of claims investigation. I just got the job a couple of weeks ago. And I'm trying to do everything by the book."

"I see."

"So I need to ask, was everything OK between you?"

"Between me and Leonard?" She looked surprised by the question. "Everything was fine. Things were always fine between us. I don't think we ever argued. Not once."

"Was he upset or depressed about anything?"

"Not that I know of." She gave me a hard look. "How would that matter?"

"Oh it's just that in a situation like this I'm supposed to rule out ...." I couldn't think of a polite way to end the sentence.

Her face went red. "Murder? Suicide?"

I nodded. "I'm supposed to rule out anything that isn't covered by your policy. Just to be sure."

"Well I certainly didn't kill him." She glared at me. "And it would be ridiculous to imagine that he committed suicide—regardless of his mood. Not in such an improbable manner as that." She'd been sitting in a chair across from me. Now she jumped to her feet. "If you read the police report, you must have read that there was a witness."

"Yes," I said. "I read it. A man named Carl Cohen saw what happened."

"Carl saw it all." There was an edge to her voice. "He was in a boat about ten yards behind us. He was following in our wake. He was looking right at us when it happened. And he corroborated my recollection of what took place in every detail."

I scratched my nose. "I take it you know him."

"Who, Carl?"

I nodded.

"Yes, I know him." Her voice began to have a tone of exasperation. "I know him quite well. Leonard knew him, too. All three of us have worked together on the radio show. Carl is the director of the show. Leonard and I have socialized with the Cohens fairly often. We're good friends. That's why they were trailing so closely behind us."

"Carl and his wife?"

"Yes. Carl and Betty."

I looked down at my lap like I was reading notes. "I understand the accident took place after sunset."

"Yes. It was dark but it wasn't completely dark. It was twilight."

I looked up at her. "Do you think there's any chance your husband might have swum ashore without being seen?"

She shook her head emphatically. "Why would he do that? We were half a mile from the shore. There were boats all around him. It would've been easy for any of the boats to pick him up. And besides ... if he'd swam ashore he'd be here, wouldn't he?"

"Maybe the knock on the head gave him amnesia."

"That's preposterous!"

"I don't think it's likely. But the problem is ... the problem is, Mrs. Lehnert, your husband's body is missing. It ought to have floated up by now. And that's the reason—really that more than anything—that I have a dilemma. Company policy says we can't pay the claim until a death certificate has been issued. And the state has yet to decide if the circumstances warrant a ruling for 'death in absentia.'" I said this in a professional tone and was quite pleased with myself, considering I'd only just learned the company's policy from my secretary Peggy that morning. Peggy had a twenty-year tenure at Amalgamated. I'd been shocked to discover how much more than me she knew about company policy. I'd asked her why Junior hadn't made her Head of Claims, given her experience. She'd said, "I'll give you one guess. It has to do with something you are that I'm not. See if you can work it out."

"What does that mean ... 'death in absentia'?" Gloria asked.

"Absent a body."

"What if his body never appears?"

"The court can declare him legally dead if his body doesn't show up ... but only after a reasonable amount of time."

"How much time?"

"It depends. The legal picture changes after seven years."

"Seven years! That's ridiculous. You don't mean to tell me the insurance won't be paid for seven years, do you?"

"Well ... there's also a condition called 'imminent peril' where the court can assume he died, even though the usual waiting time has not elapsed. I've seen that situation come up in some of our past death claims. There was one in our files where a woman died in a plane crash. They didn't find her body, but the court issued her death certificate pretty soon after the accident due to the element of peril."

"Well, who decides about the 'imminent peril'?"

"To tell you the truth, I'm not sure. Like I said, I'm still learning the ropes. I'll find out and let you know."

She nodded and sat back down in the chair opposite me. She looked around the room. "As you can imagine, Mr. Blake, this apartment comes at a very high rent. Leonard could easily afford it. He was making good money from the radio show. I have some income of my own from the show. I'm one of the writers."

"Oh, I didn't know that."

"But he was the star, and my salary doesn't even come close to his. It won't cover the cost of this place. So if it's going to take seven years before the insurance money is paid ...." She looked around again. "I'm not sure what I'm going to do."

I ran my hand through my hair. "For me, personally, I can't imagine being in a fix like that. Before I took this position as a claims investigator, I was a salesman. I sold insurance policies just like your husband's. And I can tell you, this situation is exactly what our insurance policies are made for." I stood up. "I want to do everything I can to help you. But I have to go by the book. I'll do what I can to move the investigation through as fast as I can."

"I appreciate that, Mr. Blake."

"And of course, if his body should happen to turn up … well, that would make it easier for both of us."

"Indeed."

6

———

When I got back to the office after my visit with Gloria Lehnert, I called Carl Cohen's house. His wife Betty answered and told me her husband was at the studio rehearsing for the upcoming broadcast of *The Shadow's Voice*. She repeated what Gloria Lehnert had told me, that her husband was the director of *The Shadow's Voice*.

She promised she'd telephone her husband and ask him to telephone me, which he did an hour later. I made an appointment with him to meet at five o'clock, which was when the cast and crew took a break for dinner. He said he wanted to meet me at an Italian restaurant not too far from the WGN broadcast studio in the Tribune Tower.

The restaurant was mostly empty at five, which made it easy to spot Carl Cohen, who was seated by himself at a table near the bar. I introduced myself, and explained again that I was from Amalgamated Home and Life and that I was investigating the death of Leonard Lehnert and then I sat down. He told me he'd already ordered his food and suggested I order right away in order to catch up with him.

"I'm on a schedule," he said.

I scanned the menu and ordered spaghetti, which seemed like a safe bet. "Thank you for seeing me, Mr. Cohen," I began.

"I tell you what …" He slid his chair closer to the table. "Why don't we cut the formality. You call me Carl and I call you …?"

"Elliot."

"OK, Elliot, what can I do for you? I'm a blunt person. I don't like beating around the bush. So don't hesitate to get right to the point."

"As you know, I'm here on behalf of Mr. Lehnert's life insurance company. I'm looking into the circumstances of his death. I understand you saw what happened to him."

"I saw the whole thing. I saw it plain as day. Leonard was sitting on the starboard side of *The Shadow*."

"Was that the name of his boat, *The Shadow*?"

"Yeah. *The Shadow*. They named it that for obvious reasons. The money from our show allowed them to buy it."

"And he was on the right-hand side?"

"Yes. The starboard side. His wife Gloria was at the

rudder at the back of the boat. She turned it to tack into the wind. Before she did, she called out 'coming about.'"

"You heard her?"

"Yes. You see, our boat was just a short way behind theirs. I was facing in their direction and she was facing me."

"So Mrs. Lehnert shouted 'coming about'?"

"Yes, it's the standard thing you do when you're about to change direction. And then Leonard stood up to get out of the way of the sail, but for some reason he didn't move after he got up. He just stood there. He seemed to be in a daze. He was staring past the sail out into the lake. He looked surprised by something he saw out there."

"Did you see what it was he was looking at?"

"Not right then, since I was looking at him and he was looking behind me. But moments after the accident, I did turn around and look. I couldn't see anything other than a cloud formation that was low on the horizon. Maybe the clouds looked like something else when he saw them. I don't know. Gloria said he'd had quite a few beers at that point."

"So what happened next?"

"As I said, Leonard was just standing there stupefied —looking like Lot's wife. When Gloria saw that Leonard was in the way of the boom, she swung the rudder back in the other direction. But it was too late. The wind had already caught the sail and it swung right at him. The boom hit him hard and it … it knocked him off the boat."

"Where did it hit him?"

"In the head. In the face, actually."

"Mrs. Lehnert told me her husband knew how to swim."

"I can't speak to that. Leonard and I never discussed it—and I never saw him swim. I can only tell you that after that moment when I saw him fall over the side, I never saw him again."

"So he never came back up to the surface?"

"I can't say. If he did, I didn't see him."

"You didn't notice if Mr. Lehnert was wearing boots by any chance, did you?"

"Boots?" Carl Cohen looked perplexed. "Elliot, it was a warm day for late September. The air temperature was at least 80 degrees. I'm not sure if Leonard was wearing anything on his feet at all. He might have had on boat slippers, but certainly not boots. I'd have noticed something as odd as that." Carl had eaten everything on his plate. He looked at his watch. "I'm going to have to get back to the studio soon. We only take thirty minutes for dinner."

"How are the rehearsals going?"

"To tell you the truth, Elliot, right now everything's a mess. Leonard's understudy, Freddy, has a lot of work to do. Have you ever heard the show?"

"I listen to it every week."

"Then you know that Leonard's character, Percy

Ballard, has a dual personality. Half the time he's a gossip columnist, a snob who talks like a high-society fop; the other half of the time he's a private detective who finds himself each week in the midst of a new murder case."

I nodded.

"It turns out Freddy can only do half the role. He's got the snooty gossip voice down pat—just as good as Leonard ever did it. The problem is that when he's supposed to switch to the tough guy voice, no matter how many different ways he does it, he still sounds like a flit—just with a deeper voice. At least, that's how he sounds to me. It's driving me crazy. I don't know how I missed it when I originally cast him as the understudy. I was focused on finding someone who could do the dandy voice. It never occurred to me that an actor might not be able to do the normal part."

"Why don't you use another actor?"

"It's not that easy. There's no time. The show is tomorrow night. How could I find an actor who can do both voices on such short notice?"

"Couldn't you use a different actor for the tough guy voice?"

"I can't have two different actors play the same role."

"Why not? You don't have a studio audience, do you?"

"Not for this show."

"Well … at home, no one can see who's speaking."

Carl closed his eyes, as if he was imagining what it would be like to hear the voices without seeing the actors. "Maybe," he said when he opened his eyes. "It might work. I'd have to use someone who sounds at least slightly like Freddy does. Let me think …" He sat back and closed his eyes again. After a moment, he opened his eyes and drummed his fingers on the table cloth. "I suppose I could try Roger. He's another actor in the cast. He might be able to pull it off. He'd have to come up with the right phrasing and intonation." He looked at his watch again. "You know, come to think of it, their voices *are* kind of similar." He smiled at me. "That was a good suggestion, Elliot. I think I owe you one."

I blushed. "Oh, that's OK. I'm a fan of the show."

"Right. Right." He thought for a moment. "I tell you what, we're about to rehearse. How'd you like to come by the studio and watch it? I want to give your idea a try. But I need someone to help me evaluate it. Someone neutral."

My eyes lit up. "I'd like that very much." I sat up in my seat. I hadn't expected him to suggest anything like that. Apart from a chance to see a live rehearsal of *The Shadow's Voice*, I thought about how it would give me a chance to talk to some of the other cast and crew about Leonard Lehnert. Doing so might not lead to anything, but I knew Chambers would be impressed by my thoroughness when he saw the additional interviews in my report.

"The thing is, Elliot. I need someone like you to help me assess this idea. I need someone from the regular radio audience, who can close his eyes and just listen to how it sounds. You can help me decide if your idea of using two different actors is working or not. But I don't want you to do it unless you can promise to be 100% honest about it—even if it's not working."

"Of course," I said. "I'll tell you what I hear."

"OK. Good. Then let's go to the studio."

7

The radio studio looked the way I imagined a padded cell in an insane asylum might look. There were no outside windows. The walls and ceiling were covered with perforated acoustic tiles. The back of the door was covered with the same tiles. It had the effect of making me feel like I could yell and pound the walls if I wanted to—and no one would hear me.

At one end of the studio was a plate glass window, behind which I could make out a small dark room with equipment in it. Carl told me the room was the control booth, but no one would be in it for the rehearsal. During a live broadcast, he said, a technician would sit in the booth and monitor the transmission of the show over the airwaves.

Above the control booth window was a large clock, which showed the time as 6:15. Along the opposite wall from the control booth was a Hammond organ, at which was seated a roly-poly man in a bowler hat with a mustache, a white shirt, and a red bow tie. Carl introduced the man as Alfred, who smiled and tipped his hat. I soon found that Carl called everyone in the cast and crew by his or her first name.

In one corner of the studio stood a table on which sat an odd-looking console that Carl said was the sound effects machine. Carl boasted that the machine could make any sound from the drop of a pin to the crash of a giant airplane. "It's the only one of its kind in the country," he said. "Built especially for WGN in 1936."

On the top of the console were knobs and sliders and three turntables. In the console cabinets were more switches and radio tubes and various bells and doodads and something that looked like a newsman's Speed Graphic camera. Carl told me that the sound effects man, who sat behind the console with his own microphone, was named Bob. He wore a vest and a black bolo tie like something out of the Old West. He had a merry smile and mischievous eyes. When Carl introduced me, Bob pushed a button on his console that played the sound of a telephone ringing. He winked at me and pretended to answer the telephone. "Hello," he said. "Nice to meet you, Elliot."

The actors stood in a circle around a large microphone that sat atop a heavy floor stand which bore a nameplate that read "WGN Mutual Network."

Each actor held a copy of the script for the radio play to be broadcast live the following night. Carl told me this week's episode was called "The Fortune-Teller."

Seeing the script reminded me that Gloria Lehnert had told me she was a writer for the show. "Is that one of Mrs. Lehnert's scripts?" I asked.

"Yes, it is," Carl said. "She thought I shouldn't use it this week—given the circumstances. Gloria and Leonard wrote this script together. But I figured it would be a shame to waste it. The way I look at it, Leonard is still with us tonight—in this script."

The actors gathered around the microphone included Freddy, the understudy for Leonard Lehnert, who was now going to play just one aspect of the role of Percy Ballard--the dandy voice--and Roger, who was going to have his first crack at playing the tough guy version of Percy Ballard for this rehearsal.

Carl first introduced me to Roger Trent. Roger, in a vest with a tie and jacket, was the most formally dressed man in the room. I gauged him to be around 35 years old. He had a thin black mustache and black hair that was well-doused with pomade.

Next, Carl introduced me to Freddy Foster. Unlike Roger, Freddy wore a tie but no vest or jacket. The sleeves of his white shirt were rolled up tight all the way to his biceps. He had curly brown hair and a handsome, chiseled face. His eyes, like those of the sound effects man, seemed playful. When Carl introduced us, Freddy gave me a friendly appraising look and shook my hand, which was something Roger had failed to do.

Carl then introduced me to Minnie McNally, who was the only woman and who played all the female characters on the show—always in a different voice. As a long-time listener to the show, I'd been especially looking forward to meeting Minnie in person. She wasn't the star of the show, but I loved her voice best of all.

When Carl introduced her, I shook her hand and said, "It's nice to meet you. I'm a big fan."

"You're a fan of mine?" Minnie seemed surprised.

"I love how you can handle so many characters," I said. "Your voice is always different."

"Watch out, boys," said Roger, "Minnie's got a brand new zigzag."

"I don't know," said Freddy. "I think he's totally a zag."

"In that case," said Roger, "someone should warn him that Minnie is the world's most insatiable zag lover."

"I don't understand," I said.

"Pay no attention to them, Mr. Blake," said Minnie. "They talk that way because they're jealous."

"Fat chance," said Freddy."

"We sometimes talk in code around here," Minnie continued. "It's the only way we can say mean things about Carl without him knowing it."

"Watch it, Minnie," said Carl.

"What's a zag lover?" I asked.

"It means she likes to eat little boys for breakfast," said Freddy.

"My great-uncle told me it's the best thing to cure a hangover," said Roger.

"But Minnie never drinks," said Freddy.

"Never before noon," added Roger.

"Except on days that end in y," said Alfred from across the room.

Minnie shot Alfred a dirty look. "You too, Alfred?"

"I wanted to add my little note," said Alfred, who proceeded to play a chord on the organ and then looked quite pleased with himself.

"I may enjoy the occasional drink," said Minnie. "But drinking is not my favorite thing."

"I can attest to that," said Freddy. "Minnie's favorite thing is to zig with boys who zag and have never zigged before."

"Now be nice, fellas," said Minnie. "You don't know the first thing about Mr. Blake. He seems like an upstanding young man. I'm sure he's too young to have ever zigged or zagged." She paused. "And by the way, Freddy, you know if I do zig, zigging with boys is not what I like best."

"Minnie likes everything on the menu," said Roger.

"I have a broad range of tastes," said Minnie. "For a broad, I mean. Unlike the rest of you he-men."

"C'mon now, Minnie," said Freddy. "Everyone in this room zigs or zags."

"I suppose," said Minnie. "Except Carl. He's strictly a zug."

"He's a straight down the line kind of guy," agreed Freddy. "No zig and no zag."

"What they're trying to say, Elliot," said Carl, "is that I'm the only one here who's normal. That's their idea of saying something mean about me in code." Then he held up his hand. "Now listen up, wise guys: enough cracks. It's time to get to work."

8

***

Carl sat in a chair behind a table and faced the actors. He had a copy of the script spread out on the table. Carl had informed the actors that Roger would read the role of the narrator, which was spoken in the first person and always in the tough guy voice from the point of view of the detective, Percy Ballard. I sat in a chair behind Carl, who warned me not to make a peep during the rehearsal.

Apart from the dour look on Freddy's face, the mood in the room was fairly lively. Carl clapped his hands together loudly and said, "OK. Let's take it from the top." Everyone got quiet. Carl lifted his hand like the starter at a race, then dropped it. Roger leaned close to the microphone and began to read the narration in a deadpan voice. I was surprised how low-pitched and virile Roger's voice was when he was performing. His normal speaking voice had been higher.

"My phone rang at eleven p.m.," he began, "just as I was falling asleep."

Bob played two rings of the sound effects phone.

Then Roger continued. "It was a call from a man named George Grayson. Grayson said he was calling about a domestic dispute. In my experience, calls about domestic disputes always come late in the day. It usually takes a few hours of fighting and drinking before a domestic matter gets so far out of hand that someone like me has to be awakened to have the pleasure of hearing all about it. Grayson told me I had to come see him right away because, according to him, he couldn't tell me anything over the telephone."

Roger raised the pitch of his voice slightly. "Since my eyes didn't want to stay open, I figured it might not be a good idea to drive down to see him. Instead, I decided to join the masses and take a ride on mass transit. I knew there were plenty of streetcars running, because even late at night there were plenty of eager beavers still out enjoying the nightlife."

Roger changed into a languid tone. "It was a hot night. The heat and humidity made the air thick and hazy. It made me feel like I was still asleep and having a dream." Roger paused for a beat, then continued in an ethereal tone. "A lone streetcar crawled down the street, looking like an oversized bug." As Roger spoke, Bob played the sound of a streetcar rolling on its tracks. "It was one of those new streamliner cars, the Green Hornets, they call them, the kind where the bottom half of the car is painted with a particular minty shade called 'Mercury Green' and the top half is offset with a buttery paint called 'Croydon Cream.'" Bob tapped on one of the bells in his console with a metal stick to make the ding-ding sound of a streetcar trolley bell. Roger paused for the sound, then continued: "The streetcar had a single trolley pole riding along its overhead wire that sparked whenever the trolley pole hit a gap in the wire. The spark lit up the hazy air like the flashbulb from a news reporter's camera." Bob pressed the shutter on his sound effects camera and we heard the pop of its flashbulb going off.

Roger modulated his voice, making it even more otherworldly. "The electric lights inside the streetcar illuminated a lone figure—a woman wearing a dark hat who stared vaguely out the window. I only caught a glimpse of her face, but it was the face of a goddess—a bewitching face with faraway amber eyes and silken red hair." Alfred, sitting at the organ, played an interlude of haunting music.

Roger continued: "I would have boarded that streetcar if I could have. But I was going in the other direction. I was on my way north to George Grayson's home in the Edgewater neighborhood.

"When I got to Grayson's house and looked up at the dim light bulb flickering above his front door, I had a premonition that I should never have come. When he opened the door, Grayson looked bleak."

The role of George Grayson was played by an older man named Larry. He was bald and sinewy and sounded even more like a tough guy than Roger. He stepped up to the microphone to deliver the next line in a clipped voice. "Mr. Ballard?"

"I'm Ballard."

Larry was older than Roger and his age came through in his voice, which was also gruff. "Thank you for coming, Mr. Ballard. I wouldn't have called you at this hour … but you see … well … I'm afraid my wife and I have a problem and I need your help. Please, take a seat."

"Thanks," Roger continued. "What kind of a problem, Mr. Grayson?"

"My wife has been seeing a fortune-teller. As far as I'm concerned this fortune-teller, who calls herself Madam Delilah, is a two-bit grifter. I figure the dame got into the fortune-telling racket because she knows there are plenty of women like my wife who are easy marks when they're worried about something."

"What is your wife worried about, Mr. Grayson?"

"Rose has been having what she calls premonitions. She's convinced she's going to die. How she got that idea in her head, I don't know. But Madam Delilah has only made it worse."

"Made it worse how?"

"This Delilah dame does what she calls tarot readings. Have you heard of tarot cards, Mr. Ballard?"

'Sure. I've heard of 'em. You deal the cards and they spell out your fortune."

"That's the general idea. Well, last week Madam Delilah dealt out a card she called the death card. It has a picture on it of the Grim Reaper. Ever since then Rose has been in a panic."

Larry leaned in closer to the microphone and spoke in an anxious voice. "Tonight we argued. I probably should have kept my mouth shut, but I was trying to reassure her. I told her this tarot stuff was a lot of hooey. She didn't want to hear it, so she got sore. She began to yell at me. Then she got in her car and drove away. But it's not like her to go out this late at night. I'm worried, Mr. Ballard. If you don't find Rose soon, I'm afraid it's going to be too late."

"What do you mean, 'too late?'"

"She's so distraught; she's so determined to prove she's right; I'm afraid she's going to do something stupid. Why, she might even take her own life!"

Alfred, on the organ, played a descending short bar of music similar to what an organist at the ballpark plays when the batter strikes out.

Then Roger spoke with a foreboding voice. He was really hamming it up. "Grayson, with a trembling hand, picked up a color photograph and gave it to me. What I saw made me muffle a yelp. What I saw was the face of a goddess--a bewitching face with faraway amber eyes and silken red hair."

Alfred, on the organ, again played three descending ominous notes. Then Carl stood up and said. "OK, let's stop there. Before we go on, I want to talk to Freddy about how he's going to imitate Roger's voice when he takes over in the scene with Madam Delilah."

I learned that in the next scene Ballard takes the streetcar down Clark Street to interview Madam Delilah, pretending that he's doing a story for his gossip column. For that part of the story, Percy Ballard would switch into his dandy voice, so Carl wanted Freddy to take over as Ballard, while making the audience believe that it was still Roger talking. They discussed having Freddy and Roger alternate the first few lines of dialogue with Minnie, who was playing the role of Madam Delilah, just to see if they could make the transition believable.

Roger spoke first, in his masculine, matter-of-fact voice, once again playing the role of the narrator. He said, "When I walked into Madam Delilah's salon, the first thing I noticed was her resemblance to Rose Grayson. She had the same red hair and the same color eyes, but she was ten to twenty years older. The lines on her face came through despite her thick makeup. On her sofa I saw a packed suitcase. It made me wonder if she was planning on going on a trip. I'd telephoned ahead to tell her I wanted to interview her for my column. She'd fixed herself up in all her finery and was ready to see me. She wore a turban on her head, a black lace shawl across her shoulders, and a collection of gold and silver bracelets on her wrists. Grayson told me she had a talent for dealing out tarot cards in such a way that they always painted a rosy picture. Of course with Rose, the picture had been anything but rosy. The card Madam Delilah had chosen to lay down in front of Rose was the one that spelled death!"

Alfred played another ominous chord on the organ. Now the scene switched to dialogue between Percy Ballard and Madam Delilah. Roger delivered the first line, "Well, well, I finally get to meet you. I've heard all about you, Madam Delilah."

Minnie looked more like a Hollywood starlet than a fortune-teller, but when she spoke she sounded like a world-weary sexpot with a smoky voice. She said, "Just what have you heard about me, Mister?"

Now Freddy picked up the next line from Percy Ballard. "I heard about you down at my paper. One of the beat reporters told me you have quite a little mind-reading enterprise down here. It sounds very stimulating. I write a column for the paper, you know —all about interesting goings-on around town. It's called *After Dark*." Freddy's voice, as Carl had predicted, was only slightly different from Roger's. It was similar in tone, but it had a snooty quality that Roger's voice lacked. I closed my eyes as I tried to imagine if his voice could possibly be taken as coming from the same person as Roger's voice. It seemed plausible. But I wasn't sure.

"I've seen your column. But I don't read minds, Mr. Ballard. I read tarot cards and tell fortunes. It's not the same thing at all," said Minnie as Madam Delilah.

"Oh," said Freddy, "my mistake. I guess I'm not too familiar with the racket." This time Freddy's voice sounded a bit more like Roger's. He found a gruffer tone for the sentence that ended with the word 'racket.'

"What'd ya mean *racket*?" said Minnie as Madam Delilah. "I'm strictly legit."

Now Roger jumped back in. "OK. OK. No offense. I just figured …"

'Well you figured wrong, Mister."

Freddy took over. "Well, forget that angle. As a matter of fact, I also heard about you from a friend of mine. I think you might have read tarot cards for her."

"Oh, yeah? What's your friend's name?"

"Rose Grayson."

"Rose … what? … Say …. I never heard of her."

"Oh, really. Because I was sure she must have consulted you."

"No. It must have been someone else. Now what is it you wanted to ask me about for your column, Mister Ballard?"

Now Freddy's voice took on a friendlier, less snooty tone. "Before I get to that, I couldn't help but notice that it looks like you're all packed up here. Are you going away somewhere?"

"You bet I am. I'm leaving this town for someplace warmer. It just so happens I've come into a little money lately. That's why I'm heading south." Minnie laughed. Then she said, "As a matter of fact, I came into quite a lot of money, Mister Ballard."

"What happened? Did a rich relative die and leave you money?"

"Something like that."

By the time Freddy and Roger finished alternating Percy's voice during the Madam Delilah scenes, it was evident that they were getting better at sounding like each other.

"What do you think?" Carl asked me. "Now that you've heard them, do you buy it?"

"I bought it … especially on those last few lines," I said. "I closed my eyes and didn't look at them. That helped."

"They didn't quite have it in the beginning," Carl said. "They'll have to keep working on it."

"I honestly think people will buy it," I said. "Especially if they continue imitating each other."

"Good. Good. That was a pretty useful suggestion you had, Elliot."

"So you're going to use them both?"

"Hell, at this point I don't know what else to do. It's a risk. But using Freddy for the tough guy voice would be a risk, too. He can't do it like Leonard could. We'll see how it goes on Saturday night."

It was after seven o'clock and I knew Vito would be wondering what was keeping me, so I told Carl I needed to get home. I wanted to know how "The Fortune-Teller" episode ended, but I figured I'd find out when the show aired on Saturday night.

What I didn't count on was that on Saturday night I'd be nowhere near my radio. On Saturday afternoon I got a call from Gloria Lehnert, who told me that a body the police believed was her husband's had washed up in the Chicago River. Gloria asked me if I wanted to join her at the morgue. She was going there to identify the body. I said I would meet her there.

9

I t was late on Saturday afternoon when I slogged through the rain toward the doors of the Cook County Hospital on Harrison Street. So much rain had pooled along the edge of the street that it sloshed over the top of the curb and onto the sidewalk. I stopped for a moment on a dry spot of the sidewalk to look back across the street at the Louis Pasteur memorial in Convalescent Park. Pasteur's bust gazed solemnly at the hospital from atop a stone obelisk. To me, Pasteur meant purity. Every morning I drank from a bottle of milk that declared itself to be pasteurized. So I didn't understand why the sculptor had paired Pasteur with a nude, buxom babe who was carved in stone on the right side of his monument. She stared at Pasteur from the base of the obelisk as she reached upward toward his head with a palm frond. I wasn't sure if she was getting ready to fan him or planning to smack him in the face.

I shook the rain off my hat and turned to look at the block-long hospital building in which the county morgue was housed. The building was ringed by fluted columns. Beneath the columns, open-mouthed lions sat atop portholes that were flanked by terra cotta garlands. Below the portholes were cherubs who glanced down gaily at anyone who entered, including me.

In the main lobby, the building directory indicated that the morgue was in the basement, along with the mailroom, the nuclear medicine room and the employee locker room. I took the stairs down to the basement and made my way along the hallway outside the morgue. I found an entry door next to a thick, plate glass window that looked into a room that served as the morgue office. Inside I saw Gloria Lehnert sitting on a wooden bench with her nose buried in a *National Geographic* magazine.

As I walked in, she stood up, and we shook hands solemnly. Then without speaking, we sat down side-by-side on the bench. After a short interval, a man opened an inner door, stepped into the office, introduced himself as the coroner, then turned to lead us back into the inner chamber of the morgue. The coroner was a tall, thin-haired man, who had an absent-minded, happy-go-lucky look that was at odds with the gravity of his profession. It was clear that this was all in a day's work for him.

The walls inside the morgue were subway tiles the color of false teeth and lined with huge steel lockers that I assumed held the bodies. The coroner stood next to one of the lockers and waited for us to approach.

Next to the coroner was another man, who also appeared to be waiting for us. The coroner introduced this man as Detective Thompson of the Chicago police department.

"As I told Detective Thompson," the coroner began, "it is unusual for the body of someone who drowned in Lake Michigan to show up in the Chicago River. The only way this could happen is if the body floating in the lake floated into the lock at the same time that a boat was entering the lock. Boats enter the lock frequently."

"You mean like the Wendella boats?" I asked.

"Yes," said the detective. "It might have happened when a Wendella or one of the other commercial boats that travel between the river and the lake went through. Or it could have been a private boat. Boats enter the lock from the lake end. The water level in the lock is lowered. Then the boats continue on to the river at the other end. The body could have piggybacked on the process, moving through the lock with one or more boats from the lake to the river."

"But no one saw it?" I asked.

"We found the body last night. No one reported

seeing a body in the lock," said the detective. "The boats and locks operate into the evening hours. So it's possible that the body may have moved through the lock after dark."

"Why do you think the body is that of Mr. Lehnert?" I asked.

"We found a piece of paper in the dead man's pocket with Mr. Lehnert's phone number on it. When I called the phone number, it was Mrs. Lehnert who answered. She thought it was possible that Mr. Lehnert might have kept a copy of his telephone number in his pocket."

"He could never remember it," Gloria said. "He was terrible with numbers. So he might have written it on a piece of paper."

"There was no other identification?" I asked.

"Leonard had given me his wallet and keys to put in my purse before we got out into the lake. He was worried about having them fall out of his pocket while he moved around the boat," said Gloria.

"Why did it take so long for the body to show up?" I asked.

"That's not unusual," said the coroner. "When a person drowns, the lungs, which are normally filled with air, compress as the body falls to the bottom. It can take anywhere from three to six days in warm weather for the tissue to decompose enough to create gasses inside the body that cause it to rise to the surface. Mr. Lehnert's accident was last Sunday, which was six days before the body showed up last night."

"Were you able to determine how he died?" I asked.

"The autopsy indicates that he drowned," said the coroner.

"The witness, Carl Cohen," added the detective, "has corroborated Mrs. Lehnert's account of how her husband was struck in the head by the boom of a sail, which caused him to fall into the water."

"The autopsy supports that explanation," the coroner said. "The deceased has wounds on his face that are consistent with a blow from a boom." He turned to Gloria. "So all that's left is for you to determine if this is your husband's body, Mrs. Lehnert."

"All right," said Gloria grimly.

"Are you ready, Mrs. Lehnert?" the coroner asked.

She nodded.

He opened the locker door and slid out a steel tray on which a body was covered by a white sheet, except for the feet which stuck out uncovered at the far end of the tray. As I looked at the feet, I suddenly realized I didn't have the stomach to look at the dead man's face. I'd never met the guy. I couldn't help identify him. So I took a couple of steps to the side to get out of the way. The coroner took my place, stepping in toward the head of the body. He lifted the sheet and pulled it back discreetly.

Gloria Lehnert looked down at the face below her. I

watched her. Her eyes were cold and set. She nodded and said, "That's him."

When it was clear she had nothing further to add, I decided to take a peek. I was curious to see what Vito's high school wrestling pal looked like. It was hard to tell. I could imagine that the guy had been handsome. But his hair was disheveled and his face was bruised and distorted. It was evident the body had been waterlogged. Before I had much time to examine the dead man's face, the coroner let the sheet drop and rolled the body back into the locker.

I reached out my hand with the idea that I'd pat Gloria on the back in a comforting gesture. But then I let my hand drop without touching her. I wasn't sure what to do. I felt awkward. I didn't know what my role was supposed to be in this situation beyond witnessing the fact that she'd identified the body.

Then, as if she sensed my desire to comfort her, she turned, threw her arms around me, leaned her head into my shoulder, began to whimper, and then to sob. She swayed in a way that made it seem like she might be about to keel over. I put my arm around her to steady her. I felt as if I should say something, but I was at a loss for words. After a few moments she gathered her composure, stepped back, looked up at me, and said bleakly, "I guess they'll issue his death certificate now."

"I'm sure they will," I said.

"Do I need to send you a copy? Or can you get one on your own?"

I thought for a moment, then shrugged. "I don't know." I was unsure once again about what I was supposed to do. I said, "If you wouldn't mind mailing a copy of it to our office, I'll add it to our records. Then I'm sure we can close out the paperwork and settle your claim."

She nodded. "I know this may seem strange." She hesitated, looking into my eyes as if she was checking my frame of mind. She said, "The truth is, I'm more relieved than anything else. I didn't know what I was going to do if we never found him."

"Of course." I nodded. "But now it's over. And so you can make his final arrangements."

She suddenly changed her expression. "Will you come to the funeral?" she asked.

"Oh, well," I stammered. "I don't know, Mrs. Lehnert. Do you think it's appropriate?"

"It may seem odd to ask you. But I was just thinking how it's too bad Leonard never got a chance to meet you. I'm sure he'd have liked you. You remind me of him in a way. I always said Leonard was the kind of man who put the word *gentle* in gentleman. For Leonard's sake, I'd like you to come."

I thought for a moment. "Okay," I said. "Of course." Then, as I thought more about it, I realized I didn't want to go to the funeral by myself. I wanted to bring Vito with me. I hesitated as I pondered how to phrase my request. I said, "Since you've asked me to come to the funeral, I have a favor to ask you. I was talking to a friend of mine recently about Leonard. He told me he knew Leonard in high school. My friend's name is Vito Vellucci. Maybe you know him?"

She shook her head.

"Would it be all right if I asked Vito to come to the funeral with me? He and Leonard used to be on the wrestling team together in high school."

"Oh, I didn't know." Her eyes took on an anxious look. Maybe the thought of arranging the whole thing was getting to her. She was quiet for an awkward moment, as if she was thinking it over. Finally, she said, "Of course." She smiled, regaining her composure. "Please invite your friend to come."

"Good. Once you've made the arrangements, just let me know when and where it will be." I put my hand out to shake her hand. "Good-bye."

She took my hand. "Good-bye."

She held my hand a moment, as if she was surprised I was leaving so quickly. But I had to get out of there. The air in the morgue smelled of a combination of medicinal hygiene and decay. As soon as she let go of my hand, I turned and stepped out of the inner chamber into the office, then out through the office door into the hallway. Once I got to the hallway, I started inhaling deeply to clear my nose.

I went down the hall and turned a corner. As I stepped into the elevator to go up to the main floor, I looked at my watch. *The Shadow's Voice* was going to be on the air in ten minutes. I didn't see how I could get home in time to hear it, which was too bad, since I'd hoped to hear how "The Fortune-Teller" episode ended.

I took a cab back home to Magnolia Street. I hurried into the house and into the living room. I turned on the radio. But I was too late, *The Shadow's Voice* was just ending. Roger was in the midst of reciting the closing lines of the episode in Percy Ballard's sonorous voice. Even so, I turned out the lights, like I always did when the show was on.

The only light in the room came from the streetlights. In the shadows cast through the windows of the room, I poured myself a glass of scotch and sat back in one of Winkler's wingback chairs. I should have been relaxed. The Lehnert case had cleared itself up all neat and tidy when his body turned up. Now there was nothing left to stop me from authorizing the death claim. Yet still … there was something about the case that didn't feel quite right. I just couldn't put my finger on it.

10

When Vito got home from the gym later that night he seemed unusually frisky. He grabbed me around the waist, pulled me close, and sniffed my hair. Then he cupped his hands on my butt and whispered in my ear: "You smell good."

My version of romantic banter was to put a surprised expression on my face and exclaim, "I do?"

"Yeah. You do."

I stepped back from him playfully. "I'm not wearing cologne or anything."

"Nuts to that," said Vito. "It's the smell of you I like. Not some flowery cologne. You have a smell all your own. It gets under my skin."

"Oh yeah?" I could smell him, too. And his smell, which always seemed a little sweaty, made me hot and bothered in the same way. I wobbled back toward him.

"Have you been drinking?" he asked.

"A little … I had some scotch. Not a lot. How can you tell?"

"You're a little rickety on your feet."

"Maybe I am."

"What brings this on?"

"It's this Lehnert case," I said. "Gloria identified his body."

"Did she?"

"Yes, and now I can officially pay the claim. I suppose it's over, but it doesn't feel over. Something still feels off about it."

He nodded. "I hate to say it, but something *is* off about it." He patted my arm. "I've got something to tell you." He let go of me, made his way over to the liquor cabinet, got out the scotch bottle, and poured himself a drink.

"Tell me what?" I asked.

He took a sip from his drink. "The strangest thing happened just now. I was on my way home from the gym. I was walking down Clark Street when I saw a streetcar pass by. I saw a man sitting in the window of the streetcar who was staring at me."

"People are always giving you the eye. Both men and women, I've noticed."

"The man in the streetcar was Leonard Lehnert."

"Come on, Vito. That's impossible."

"He was on the 22 Clark. He was wearing a hat. He

had his collar turned up. But even from a distance, I could tell it was him."

"It couldn't have been him. I just got back from the morgue a couple of hours ago. His wife was there. She identified his body. I saw him … all covered up by a sheet."

"Well then, maybe there are two people with the same name. Because the Leonard Lehnert I knew in high school was riding in a streetcar down Clark Street fifteen minutes ago. And from the way he looked at me, I could tell he recognized me, too."

"But you said you haven't seen him in a decade."

"Until today, I hadn't. It's odd, don't you think, that now's the first time I'd see him in all these years, just when this crazy case of yours comes along?"

"Maybe it wasn't him. Ten years is a long time."

"It's not *that* long. He looked older. But he still looks basically the same. In fact, he looked pretty good."

"What's that supposed to mean?"

"I told you he was good-looking, Elliot. I'm just saying he hasn't lost his looks. That's all. And, you know—a guy like that, he catches your eye. That's how I happened to see him."

"He caught your eye?"

"Yeah."

"Riding by in a streetcar?"

"Well. Yeah."

"So you were just out walking, looking for handsome men along the way?"

"Oh, for God's sake. I was walking home from the gym. Just because you and I are living together doesn't mean I stop noticing other people when I run across them."

"I see."

"And don't play innocent with me. I've seen your eyes glance here and there, checking out this one and that one when we're together. And why not? Hell, man, that's how it is. People are like that. Well, men are, anyway."

"OK. OK. Fine." I could feel myself getting sore about it. But I knew it wasn't really Vito I was sore about. It was Leonard Lehnert. I made myself calm down. I said, "So like you say, maybe there are two guys with the same name."

"Maybe."

"And maybe there's a way we can find out."

Vito looked skeptical. "How?"

I wasn't sure how Vito would react to the idea of going to the funeral, so I just blurted it out. "Mrs. Lehnert invited me to Leonard's funeral. I asked her if it would be OK if I brought you along. She said it was fine."

"Jesus, Elliot. I don't want to go to a funeral."

"I told her you knew him. And I thought you'd want to go."

"Why would I want to go?"

"Because you were friends in high school."

"We weren't really friends. Besides, the guy who's dead is probably not the guy I knew."

"Well, then, all the more reason I need you to come with me."

"Why?"

"So you can have a look at the corpse and verify that it's not the man you knew in high school."

"Really? You think there could be any other explanation than that it's someone else? I just saw the man."

"Well, I think you think you saw him. But if you come with me to the funeral and have a look at the body in the coffin, you're gonna be able to make up your mind which one is the Leonard Lehnert you knew —the guy in the streetcar or the guy in the casket."

"I'm sure the streetcar guy was the guy I knew from high school. And like I told you before, it doesn't fit that the Leonard I knew would be married. He was the same as me and you. He liked the boys more than the girls. I'm sure of that, too. Why would he get married?"

"Guys do."

Vito looked exasperated. "Maybe."

I thought for a moment. "Didn't you tell me that Leonard was in the theater club in high school?"

"Yeah, he was. So what? You think he's just playing the part of a dead man?"

"Look, Vito. Mr. Zimmerman told me he'd get a feeling about things like this whenever something didn't seem right. He always had an intuition. And one thing he used to warn me about was coincidence. He said one coincidence is normal. But when there are lots of coincidences; that's not normal. He said a lot of coincidences mean somebody's up to something."

"Maybe." Vito nodded. "But what good does it do for a man who's not dead to pretend to be dead."

"The insurance claim."

"Oh." Vito closed his eyes as he pondered this.

"It's a lot of money," I said.

"Yeah … I suppose it is." Vito opened his eyes. "So you're saying she identified the body, but it might not really be her husband's body?"

"Right." I nodded. "I guess that's what I mean."

"So then, if her husband was riding the streetcar on Clark Street while you and she were down at the morgue, whose body did you see on that slab at the morgue? Whose body is going to be in that coffin at the funeral home?"

I suddenly remembered something. "Wait a minute." I held up my hand. "I'll be right back." I ran up the stairs to our bedroom. I'd brought the Lehnert case file home from work. The case file was on the bedroom dresser. I grabbed it and ran back down the stairs.

"This is the file on Lehnert," I said. "Before I left work Peggy told me she'd added something to the file: a newspaper clipping from an article in the *Tribune* about *The Shadow's Voice*. She mentioned that the clipping included a photo of Lehnert. I brought the file home, but I haven't had a chance to look at it yet." I opened the file and shuffled through the papers until I found the clipping. I held it up. "Here it is."

Vito and I both stared at it for a moment. Then we said in unison, "That's him!"

"Wait," I said. "What do you mean that's him? You mean the man in the photo is the kid you knew in high school?"

"Yeah. That's definitely him. And he's the same man I saw on the streetcar. Why? What do you mean?"

"I mean that's the face of the man I saw in the morgue."

Vito shook his head. "It can't be. Are you sure?"

"I'm as sure as you seem to be about whoever you saw on the streetcar." I rubbed my forehead. I was beginning to get a sense of how difficult this was going to make things for me. I didn't see how I could approve Gloria's claim. But what reason could I give her? I stared at the photo in the clipping. I said, "I only got a quick look at the dead man's face. But the face I saw looked to me the way the man in this photo would've looked if he'd been floating in Lake Michigan for a week. His face was bruised—and he was definitely waterlogged—but he looked like this photo." I jabbed my finger at the photograph in annoyance.

"I think I will come to that funeral," Vito said. "One of us has to be wrong. I think the only way we can settle this is by taking a look at the body inside that coffin."

11

———————

Leonard Lehnert's funeral took place at Moran's Funeral Home. Vito and I got to Moran's early. We brought the newspaper clipping with us so that we could take it to the coffin before the other mourners arrived and make a direct comparison. But as it turned out, we needn't have brought the clipping. On a table in the foyer sat a guest book. Next to it was a framed black and white print of the same photograph of Leonard Lehnert that was in the clipping. It was a glossy publicity photo from *The Shadow's Voice*. Gloria Lehnert had the original.

While I was looking at the photograph, Vito poked me in the side and nodded toward the set of glass doors in the foyer that opened to the interior of the funeral parlor. It took a minute for my eyes to adjust. The interior room was dark since all the windows inside were covered by heavy crimson drapes that fell onto an oriental carpet which ran from wall to wall. Oversized floor lamps with dark red shades stood in each corner emitting a shadowy light. The only other light in the room came from a spotlight hanging from the ceiling that lit up the casket.

That's when I saw why Vito poked me. "Oh, no," I said. The casket lid was closed. And on top of the lid was a wreath of red flowers.

Gloria Lehnert stood next to the sign-in book waiting to receive mourners. She was dressed in a black satin dress trimmed with black fur. She looked at me just as I said 'Oh, no,' as if she heard what I said. Instinctively, I pulled on Vito's arm and we took a few steps away from her.

"Now what?" I muttered.

"Maybe they'll open it later," he whispered.

I made a face. "Do you really think that once everyone is seated they're gonna pull that wreath off the top and flip up the lid?"

"I guess we should have expected this."

"Seeing how the body is so waterlogged," I said, "I suppose they had no choice."

Vito shrugged. "Maybe when everyone leaves we can take a peek inside."

I wondered if Vito understood how funerals work. "Have you been to a funeral before?"

"As a matter of fact, no. I don't go to funerals. I'm only here now because of you."

"At the end of the service the pallbearers will go up

to the casket and pick it up. Then they'll carry it out to a hearse. Then everybody will ride to the cemetery in a procession of cars following the hearse. Then as soon as they get to the cemetery, they'll lower the coffin into the ground and throw dirt on it."

"OK," Vito said. "I get it. Once the service starts, there won't be an opportunity to peek inside the casket." Vito pulled me further away from Mrs. Lehnert and turned me around so my back was to her. He whispered, "So how about if we do it right now?"

'What! She's standing right there."

"Yeah, but no one else is here yet. You distract her and I'll go in and pop open the lid and take a quick look."

"Distract her how?"

"Get her to turn and look out the front window—so her back is to the interior. Or maybe you can get her to step outside."

"How?"

"I don't know. Think of something. I'm going in."

Before I could object, Vito walked into the interior room. I coughed loudly as if I was clearing my throat and lurched toward Mrs. Lehnert. "Oh, no," I said, touching her arm. "I think it's going to rain."

Startled, she looked at me as if I was crazy. "I don't think so."

"No, really." I tugged on her arm. "Come out for a minute and have a look at the sky."

"What does it matter?"

My mind was racing. "You'll need an umbrella. I can get you one."

"There's no rain in the forecast."

Now I practically pulled her arm. "No, really. You should look. See what you think. You should be prepared." My voice was pleading. "I can get you an umbrella," I said again.

She tilted her head, then reluctantly followed me out the door. When we got outside, she looked up. I turned to look back inside, but I couldn't see what Vito was doing.

"There are hardly any clouds at all," she said. "I don't see what you're talking about."

"Oh?" I said, as if I was suddenly confused. "I swear there were rain clouds blowing in just when we got here."

"Well," she said, "there aren't any now."

Just then a group of four mourners arrived, two couples. Mrs. Lehnert embraced each of them one by one and they spoke a few words in solemn tones. Then all five proceeded into the foyer. To keep her attention focused outside, I stayed outside and knocked on the window. "Mrs. Lehnert!" I exclaimed. "If you want an umbrella, just let me know."

"Mr. Blake, I really don't think it will be necessary." She spoke with irritation.

Vito emerged by himself through the interior glass doors and stepped back into the foyer. I walked back inside. "Vito," I said, as if I'd been looking for him.

"There you are." I pulled him over to a far corner of the foyer.

He looked at me solemnly. "I don't think the body in the casket is the Leonard Lehnert that I knew," he said. "I don't see how it could be him."

"Did you get a good look?"

"Good enough. And I admit, the body in the coffin does look a lot like Leonard."

"The body was soaking in the lake for days."

"It doesn't matter. I checked his anatomy. It wasn't big enough."

"You did what?"

"Well … " Vito cleared his throat. "I reached in and slid my hand down the inside of the deceased's trousers."

"Oh, for Christ's sake. Vito!" My voice was louder now, and I didn't care. "You reached inside his pants?"

"Keep it down," Vito said. "Yeah. I had to be sure."

"That's creepy."

"What does it matter? The guy's dead."

"And that's how you know it wasn't Leonard Lehnert? I thought you said you never touched him down there."

"I didn't have to. When Leonard was in his wrestling singlet, I saw what everyone else saw. He wasn't shy about it."

"But what about his face? You said it looked like him."

"The man *does* look like him."

I tried to think of an explanation. "Maybe spending a week underwater caused his anatomy to shrink," I said.

Vito shrugged. "I don't know."

"What am I supposed to do with this?" I looked around. The foursome had drifted now into the interior room. I leaned into Vito's ear. "How'm I gonna put something like this in my report?"

Vito drew his fine dark brows together in thought. Then he said, "Beats me."

I looked out the foyer window and saw a group of five more people making their way in a single file toward the door of the funeral parlor. The group consisted of most of the cast and crew from *The Shadow's Voice*. Only Carl Cohen was missing from the group.

First in the line was Alfred, the organist. He had on his black bowler hat, a black suit, and a black bow tie. Following Alfred was Bob, the sound effects man, wearing his bolo tie, but this time with a black suit coat. Gone was his impish expression, replaced by a suitably somber face. After Bob came Roger, who wore a three-piece dark suit and no hat. He also wore his characteristic sneer and plenty of pomade in his hair. Despite the ointment, his cowlick was sticking up from the back of his scalp. That explained why he used so much grease. The poor guy clearly had no idea that his ointment wasn't working. The tuft of hair looked like a radio antenna in the back of his head.

After Roger came Minnie, the woman who'd played Madam Delilah at the rehearsal. She wore a black suede dress, a black hat with a veil, and black patent leather high heel pumps. The well-fitted dress accentuated her curves. Its voluptuousness seemed at odds with the formality of the occasion. I'd noticed how much stage presence her voice had had in the studio. She knew how to conjure up a lot of physical presence as well, when she wanted.

Next came Freddy, who was wearing a flecked tweed grey suit and a black shirt with a white tie. Like Minnie's dress, his suit was made-to-fit. And it fit tight enough to emphasize his shoulders, his chest, and especially his skinny waist. The moment Freddy saw us, he stopped walking. He stood six feet back with his eyes wide as he stared at Vito. Then he walked straight up to Vito, and jabbed at his shoulder, "You!?"

Vito looked up just as Freddy touched him. "Frederick!" he said with obvious surprise.

"What are you doing here?" Freddy demanded.

"Me? What about you?" replied Vito.

"You two know each other?" I tried to step in between them.

"Frederick and I go way back," Vito said. "We were in school together."

Freddy turned his attention to me, then spoke to Vito. "It looks like you and detective boy here have met," he said.

"I'm not actually a detective," I said. "I'm a claims investigator for the insurance company."

"Elliot is handling Mrs. Lehnert's death claim," Vito added. "That's why we're here."

"I get why he's here," said Freddy. "But what about you?"

"I'm here because Elliot and I are buddies."

"Buddies, eh?" Freddy made the word full of innuendo. "I see." He glanced at me. "Now it all makes sense." He turned back to Vito. "You know, Vito, I can see where Elliot might be the buddy-boy type. But not you, Vito. I never figured you as the type of guy who'd let himself get that cozy with anyone."

Vito looked amused. "Maybe it's because I never met the right buddy-boy before."

"What are you two talking about?" I asked.

"Frederick and I are just going over some ancient history," Vito said. "There was a time when Frederick here had the idea that he might be my buddy. But then I discovered he was out to sabotage me."

"And what about you?" Freddy shouted. "You're the one who dropped me like a hot potato."

"Yes I did!" Vito shouted back. "And you know exactly why I did. I asked you nicely. I begged you to be good. But you couldn't help yourself."

"Well how was I supposed to know your Petty Officer had a vendetta against you? I didn't think he could ever prove anything—not from the things I wrote. I was just being funny."

"Look, Frederick, I don't want to go back over this. It's water under the bridge." Vito made an obvious effort to lower his voice. "So let's not get all in a stew. This is a funeral. Show some respect."

"Fine."

"I still would like to know why you're here," Vito said quietly.

"Don't you ever listen to the radio, Vito?" Freddy lowered his voice, and it was full of bitterness. "That's why I'm here. Leonard and I are the stars of a little show called *The Shadow's Voice*. Carl's the director. You remember Carl, don't you? It's the number one show on Saturday night. It's on WGN. Jesus, Vito, where've you been? Does any of this ring a bell?"

"Elliot mentioned it," Vito said. "But it's not my kind of show. Anyway, I've never listened to it."

"Then what's the point of you being here?" Freddy asked. "Is it just because you came with your buddy?"

"Yeah, and because, as you well know, once upon a time Leonard and I were friends. I came to pay my respects."

"Some friend you are," said Freddy.

The exchange between Vito and Freddy had me thoroughly confused. I had to stop myself from interrogating Vito about what it all meant. I had no idea that Vito had known Freddy. And from the way Freddy talked about him, he implied that Vito knew Carl as well.

"It's getting crowded in here," Vito said, loud

enough for Freddy to hear. To me, he said, "Let's step outside for a minute."

I looked around the room, which was quickly filling up. A priest stood behind the podium that had been placed behind Leonard's casket. The priest was studying sheets of paper he'd laid out on the podium. I knew from the file that Leonard was Catholic. I assumed the priest was reviewing notes for the eulogy.

Gloria Lehnert was standing just to one side of the coffin and talking to another priest.

"OK, Vito," I said. "Let me just say something to Mrs. Lehnert. Then we can go if you want."

Vito looked at Gloria and at the priest she was talking to. He frowned and turned around to face away from them. "You talk to her," he said. "I'm going outside."

I interrupted Gloria Lehnert's conversation with the priest long enough to tell her that something had come up and that I couldn't stay for the rest of the funeral. I promised her I'd be in touch with her soon about her claim.

After that, Vito and I walked out of the funeral parlor. I could tell that Vito, in his tamped-down way, was fuming.

12

s soon as we were outside Moran's funeral parlor, I stopped and turned to face Vito. "What the hell was that all about?"

"Forget it."

"You knew those guys in school—both Freddy *and* Carl?"

"Sure. I knew them."

"What did Freddy mean about you and him being buddies and ..." I paused as my mouth went dry. "... and about you dropping him like a hot potato?"

'Look, Elliot. Frederick is ...." Vito searched for the word he wanted. "He can be a jerk sometimes. But, yeah, there was a time when he and I were pals."

"What kind of pals?"

"The kind like you and me." The anger rose in Vito's voice. "I know you're not as slow on the draw as you pretend to be."

My mouth was still dry. I drew my lips and made a half-hearted attempt to lick them. "What do you expect? You never talk about any of your friends from the past."

"As far as I'm concerned, my life is an open book!"

"That's not true. How do you know Carl? You've never mentioned him."

"Carl … ?" Vito shrugged. "I met him in college, at the same time I met Frederick. It was before the war."

"At the University of Chicago?"

"Yes, at U of C. We were all classmates."

"What about Leonard?"

"He went to the University of Michigan. I never saw him after high school."

"So what happened? You and Freddy and Carl just fell out of touch?"

"Yeah. We did. Because when the war started, I went into the service and they didn't."

"How'd they manage that?"

"They both got a deferment. Carl's was for a medical condition. Frederick, on the other hand, made himself ineligible. When they asked him if he liked girls, he said, 'no.'"

I thought about what that meant. I knew from my own experience that answering the question that way took courage. I said, "That was brave."

"Yeah. It took guts. I'll give him that."

I grew quiet as I remembered my own induction interview. "They asked me the same thing."

"Me, too." Vito said. "They asked every guy that question. And since I know you were inducted, I know you answered it the same way I did."

"When they asked me, I couldn't understand what they were getting at. I thought it was a trick question."

"Well, the trick was if you said, 'no,' you automatically got a 4-F deferment. Most 4-Fs were for medical or physical problems. But they also gave 4-Fs for moral and character issues. And they put a note in your record spelling out exactly what your immoral defect was. Then good luck getting a job after that."

"Freddy got a job," I pointed out. "He's a radio actor."

"It might not matter for actors. But picture me getting a shot at boxing if they knew I was like that."

"But you are like that."

"Yeah, Elliot. I am." He smiled prettily. "And aren't you glad I am?" He seemed to have brought his anger fully under control. He had an ability to do that.

"So why did you and Freddy break up?"

"Like I said, I was drafted. He wasn't."

"But you said he tried to sabotage you. And he said you dropped him like a hot potato."

"During the war, Freddy wrote me some things he shouldn't have. At the same time, he was also beginning to get, uh ... clingy and jealous. I didn't like it." He said this coolly, but I felt the sting of it all the same. There was no doubt I'd behaved in the same way when I thought he was seeing Margo.

"For the record, I … I can't help it if I sometimes get jealous, too. I don't know why."

"I don't know, either." He gazed at me as if he were giving me the once-over one more time. "Damn it, Elliot, for a guy who's as good-looking and nice as you are, you sell yourself short."

I nodded.

"And the trouble is," Vito continued, "it has the opposite effect from the effect you want."

"What does that mean?"

"It means jealousy bugs the hell out of me."

"I know it does," I said. "I'm sorry."

"There's something else I should tell you."

I felt my body tense. But I kept my voice calm when I said, "Tell me."

"Did you notice the priest that Mrs. Lehnert was talking to right before we left?"

"Sure. I saw him."

"The priest's name is Father Whalen. He was a chaplain at the naval base in Pearl Harbor when I was stationed there."

"You're kidding? You know him?"

"Not exactly. Let's just say I recognized him. I remember him because he made a creepy move on me when I was in the library on base."

"The priest?"

"Yeah. Like I said, he was a chaplain back then. He was very sly about it. He was supposed to be somebody I could trust."

"What happened?"

"Nothing. It started the same way as with Walt Winkler. The guy wanted me. But in this case nothing happened. Fortunately, he didn't have anything on me the way Winkler did."

"Did he say something to you at the funeral?"

"No. He looked like he was all wound up about something with Mrs. Lehnert. He barely glanced at me."

"Maybe he didn't remember you," I said.

"It's not surprising," Vito said. "The way I figure it, he probably tried his moves on a lot of sailors during the war. Tonight, when he saw me out of uniform, I could tell he didn't remember me. But I sure as hell remembered him."

I felt a surge of relief to realize that Vito's 'something else' had nothing to do with my jealousy. "Gosh," I said, "So many surprises from your past."

"Yeah. The funeral was full of 'em."

"I wonder what a guy like that priest was doing at Leonard's funeral."

"Beats me," said Vito. "But I didn't want to stay long enough for him to remember me. That was another reason I wanted to leave."

I looked around and realized we'd walked several blocks from the funeral home. I suddenly felt tired of walking. "What do you say we get a cab?"

"A cab? You're kidding. I've never been in a cab in my life!"

"There's nothing to it, Vito. I took a cab for work just last week, when I visited Mrs. Lehnert. It's easy. You just wave your hand in the air and one of them stops."

"I know how it works." Vito looked around to get his bearings. "But do you really want to spend the money? We're only a mile and a half from home."

"I'm tired."

"OK. Fine." Vito put his hands in his pocket. "I guess you're a big shot now. Have it your way."

I stepped over to the curb on the corner. I acted like I knew what I was doing. I raised my hand above my head and twirled my forefinger assertively. A cab came along. Evidently the driver decided I did know what I was doing. He pulled over, and Vito and I climbed in. I sat on one side of the back seat and Vito sat on the other. I looked at the eyes of the driver in the rear view mirror to see if he was watching us.

Maybe if Vito or I had as much guts as Freddy had in front of his draft board, we'd have let ourselves sit closer together. I let my hand flop on the seat. I was pretty sure my hand was below the driver's field of vision in the mirror. I began to inch it toward Vito. I got my hand to the point where I was almost touching Vito's leg. Vito turned and looked at me. He made a face and grunted. "You're just like that priest," he said. He swatted my hand away like he might swat away an annoying fly.

I knew it wasn't fear of the cab driver that made him do it. He did it partly out of primness. But I think mostly he did it because of the jealousy he sensed in me.

13

The evening after Leonard Lehnert's funeral, when I got home from work, I was alone in the house. Vito was at the gym. He usually went to the gym on Monday afternoon. But he went in late because he was giving boxing lessons to a kid who needed pointers, and evening was the only time the kid could meet.

Meanwhile, I was killing time. I was lying on the sofa in the living room, staring at the ceiling, and brooding about what I'd learned about Vito's past. The wiser part of me knew there was no point in being jealous of Freddy. Any idiot could see that in the present there was nothing between them. If anything, they appeared to loathe each other. So why was I wary?

Maybe it was because I kept picturing how seductive Freddy looked in his jazzy, flecked tweed suit. He'd worn a thin black belt that was just tight enough and high enough on his waist to accentuate his assets.

And maybe it was because I knew there *had* been something between them in the past. I couldn't stop myself from obsessing about whether the physical and emotional attraction that had brought them together in the past might reawaken now that they'd run into each other. What if sparks began to fly again?

All my life I'd heard the expression, "let sleeping dogs lie." I should have heeded that advice. But I couldn't help myself. I was alone. Vito would be at the gym for quite a while. And I was certain that a sleeping dog was lying upstairs in the back of the closet in our bedroom.

Before I could think better of it, I found myself climbing the stairs with the intention of waking up that dog so I could learn his secrets. The dog was a Pendaflex file storage box that Vito kept on a shelf in the back of the bedroom closet. It wasn't exactly concealed on the shelf, but it was obscured by a pile of Vito's workout clothes, which he kept in a stack in front of it.

I'd first found the storage box on another day while Vito was at the gym. I'd pulled some of Vito's workout jerseys down from the shelf to try them on. Vito would have thought it weird for me to wear his clothes. But I'd told myself it was the sort of thing anyone in love might do—so why not?

It was after I'd pulled down his clothes that I saw the box, which was dusty because it hadn't been touched for so long. It was made of marbled black and white binder board and had a curved orange spine with the word "Letters" printed on it. I didn't touch it. But the vision of it sitting there stuck in my mind.

Now, as I was climbing the stairs, I told myself that since Vito had put the letter box in a spot that was out of the way but not hidden, he must not have had any reason for me not to know about it. When I'd accused him after the funeral of never talking about his past, he'd said, "That's not true, I'm an open book"—which to me said he had no problem with being totally candid about his past.

And that was how … bit by bit … I talked myself into going upstairs, walking into the bedroom, opening the closet door, taking down the folded pile of jerseys, and then standing on the tips of my toes in order to reach the Pendaflex box.

I took it out of the closet and set it on the bed. I sat down next to it and stared at it for a long while. I fixed my gaze on the small suitcase-style clasp on the back of the box. Finally, I took a breath and opened the clasp. Inside I saw two bundles of envelopes with rubber bands around them. The envelopes in one of the bundles bore stamps, postmarks and return addresses. The other bundle contained envelopes that were labeled with handwritten dates and had no stamps.

I pulled the rubber band off the bundle of stamped

envelopes and chucked the letters onto the bed haphazardly. I scanned them to be sure they were all addressed to Vito. They were. I noticed that Vito's address changed over time. The letters with the earliest postmarks were addressed to Vito at an address in Hyde Park. I assumed that was the address where he'd lived before he'd enlisted, when he was first going to school as an undergraduate at the University of Chicago. The next letters chronologically were addressed to Vito at the Naval Base at Pearl Harbor, Hawaii. Vito had been a sonar technician on a submarine during the War. I assumed he'd been sent to the base in Hawaii for training before he shipped out.

I arranged the Hyde Park letters into a pile. They all bore the name "Frederick Foster," written in the return address. I looked at the postmarks. The earliest one was from October 10th, 1939. The last one was postmarked December 20th, 1941.

The date of that last postmark rang a bell. That was the day the Selective Service Act was amended to make all men between the ages of twenty and forty-four liable for military service. Before that amendment, the government was only drafting men twenty-one and over. I remembered the date because my buddy Maurice had turned twenty that year and the new act had made him eligible for the draft for the first time. He'd called me up in a panic on December 20th to ask me what I thought he should do.

A lot of guys began to lie about their age. Some

pretended to be older than they really were so they could enlist. That's how eager some guys were to get out there and kill Nazis. But not Maurice. Maurice didn't want to kill anybody. And he certainly didn't want anyone killing him. I didn't have any advice for Maurice. I didn't think there was anything he could do.

As it turned out, I was wrong. Maurice got out of the draft by qualifying for a 4-F deferment due to stammering. Apparently another of his confidants had told him about this particular angle. I'd never known Maurice to stammer at any time during his entire life. But apparently throughout his draft board interview he stammered like a broken record. He stammered so forcefully they could barely make out what he was saying. According to him, the written statement from his draft board said he was judged to be unable to express himself clearly or repeat commands. And that qualified him for 4-F.

I had mixed feelings about the draft. I was no more eager than Maurice to put on a uniform and face a bunch of Nazis pointing guns at me. But after Pearl Harbor there was no way I was gonna stand by and not do something. Like a lot of guys, if I thought about it at all, I told myself the odds were I'd come out OK. Mostly I didn't think about it. I registered for the draft in 1940. But due to my lottery number, I didn't get inducted until the week after Pearl Harbor in 1941.

That was the week the army began mailing out "Greetings" letters by the truckload.

I knew that Vito and Freddy had been classmates at the University of Chicago, which meant they were roughly the same age. The day in December when the 1941 amendment became law would have been the day they both knew for sure they were going to be inducted. Since that was the date of the last letter Freddy wrote to Vito at his address in Hyde Park, I figured it must have been a turning point with them.

In addition to the Hyde Park letters, the bundle of stamped letters in the storage box included four more letters from Freddy addressed to Vito, care of the Naval Base at Pearl Harbor. I put these in a separate pile. The dates on those letters ranged from July, 1942 to November, 1943.

The second bundle of envelopes were all plain white envelopes. Each was labeled with a date between 1939 and 1942. They had no stamps and had never been sealed. I picked up the first one and opened it. Inside was a hand-written letter. The letter was dated June 18, 1942, and began "Dear Frederick." I quickly flipped the letter paper over and saw at the end of the letter it was signed 'Your pal, Vito." I instantly turned red.

I stopped myself from reading it. I opened the remaining envelopes in the second bundle. All of them were letters from Vito to Freddy. Apparently Vito had either kept first drafts of his letters or made copies of them before he mailed them. I felt that if I read the letters that Vito wrote, I'd be invading his privacy even more than by reading the letters that Freddy wrote. I wasn't ready to go that far. I put all of the letters that Vito wrote back into their envelopes and put the rubber band back around the bundle. I set it aside. I wasn't ready to betray Vito's trust to that degree.

I was, however, ready and willing to read the letters that Freddy wrote. Using my own crazy logic, I reasoned that Freddy's personal correspondence was fair game. I didn't know him. I wasn't hoping to develop a close relationship with him. His letters were just an historic relic, an archive that happened to be in the back of our closet. Vito had told me that he was an open book. And I was only naturally curious to enlarge my knowledge of history.

I knew I was going to read Freddy's letters, but I wasn't sure where to begin. Part of me wanted to start by opening the October 10th, 1939 letter, so I could follow the progress of Freddy's correspondence with Vito in chronological order. Another part of me was bursting to find out what Freddy wrote on December 20th, 1941 when he and Vito both knew they'd have to face the music from the draft.

Before I did anything, I decided to go down to the living room where Vito kept all the liquor bottles. At this point I knew I was starting down a bad path. I poured four fingers of Old Crow rye whiskey into what Vito referred to as a 'rocks glass.' I didn't add any rocks. I downed the entire glass in one gulp.

I walked back upstairs and opened the December, 1941 letter. This is what I read:

December 20, 1941

Dear Vito,

I know you won't like this, but I've decided I'm going to tell the draft board I'm queer. I want to be done with it. It's not because I'm afraid of going to war. I hope you know that. Hell, I wish there was a way I *could* go. I'd make as good a soldier as any man. But I'm not about to put myself in a situation where I have to lie and pretend for months on end to be something I'm not. I just can't do it.

I can't shower with them, use the latrine with them, sleep in the barracks with them, have drinks in the canteen with them. I can't do any of it. After two days of being around all those horny men, I'd get so nervous worrying about where my eyes were wandering and wondering how my voice sounded that I'd end up turning into a parody of myself. I'd be forever holding my wrist rigid. My eyes would probably get stuck looking at the heavens to avoid looking at their bodies. My throat would probably go dry from forcing my voice to be an octave lower. I'm not kidding.

I couldn't pull it off. Besides, I just don't want to.

It's one thing to be always looking over my shoulder for the vice squad to come busting in or waiting for bashers to jump out of the bushes in order to attack me. But imagine if I had to constantly watch out for MPs, who were ready to throw me in the brig, court-martial me, discharge me with dishonor, and God knows what they would do to my civilian life. Who could I trust in the army? At least with our gang we all know what's what, who we are, who we can talk to, and who we can't.

So when the draft board examiners ask me if I like girls I'm going to say 'no.' The irony is, I do like girls. If I was going to tell them the truth, I'd tell them the only time I ever really feel comfortable is around girls. I think Minnie is my best friend. Minnie's not the girliest girl, but she's got a woman's heart. Men, for the most part, are a bunch of louts. Except you, of course, sweetheart. You're just a big lunk with a hunk of mush for a heart.

You don't have to fret. I won't mention your name. Hell, I'll act like I don't even know you. As far as the draft board psychiatrist is concerned, my story will be that I only ever get queer on Tuesday afternoon in the men's room at Marshall Fields. And for the record, I know that's a plausible story because I actually did do something naughty there once, with a salesman from—get this—Peacock Jewelers. Don't worry baby, Mr. Peacock had nothing on you.

The reason I'm writing to you instead of telling

you about this in person is because I don't want to get into a big fight. I know you, Mr. Tough Guy. I figure you're planning to run over to the draft board next week with your boxing gloves on yelling 'sign me up!' or 'let me at 'em' or something to that effect.

Seriously, when they ask you if you like girls, you should at least say something like "I can take 'em or leave 'em." Give the man some element of the truth. Hell, who am I kidding? The doc will take one look at you and he most likely won't even ask you the question for fear you might punch him out.

The way I figure it, I'm going to be leading a civilian life in 1942 doing God knows what, while you'll get to go bivouacking with the boys in some military shithole. Knowing you, you'll lie there in your pup tent as cool as a cucumber without a care in the world while you confidently wait for some hapless Mr. Hotsy Totsy to sneak into your tent. Then you'll do him the honor of adjusting your trousers so as to allow him to get his mouth just where you want it.

Do I sound bitter? Maybe I am. I don't like anything about this situation. Not the war. Not the draft. Not Hitler. Not the Nips. Not the Krauts. Not having to strip and sit in a chair and tell some tight-assed doctor that I'm a panty-waist. Not losing you for God knows how long. The whole fucking world has gone to hell and there's not a damn thing I can do about it.

But the truth is, my friend, I love you. And remember, Vito, ever since that day on the Midway Plaisance at the Fountain of Time when I first told you, 'I love you,' I've always stayed true to you. Well, except for that one time at Marshall Fields. See, I can't help being a bitch.

I don't know how to avoid being separated from you. I just want to be with you. And I want you to be safe.

Your loving friend,
Fred

14

I was in a daze when I finished reading Freddy's letter. I'd had no idea that the relationship between Vito and Freddy had been so serious. From the beginning I'd assumed the two of them had had sex. That alone had been difficult for me to accept. But I thought, so what? Every guy has done some fooling around at a certain point in his life. I'd certainly done my share of fooling around before I met Vito. What I hadn't contemplated was that Vito and Freddy might actually have been in love. Somehow I'd imagined that when Vito appeared in my life at age twenty-eight, he'd arrived without any kind of romantic past. Before I met him I hadn't even considered that two men might be in love with each other, let alone use the words 'I love you' in writing. And when I found myself saying it to Vito, no one was more surprised than I was.

But now everything fell into place. How could I not have known? Of course Vito had already had a lover. Now I said it out loud, "Hell, he must have had lots of them." And it pained me to realize the truth of it. I couldn't control my jealousy, which coursed through me like venom. I tried.

I sat on the bed for more than twenty minutes fighting the compulsion to keep reading. The words written in Vito's hand "Dear Frederick" floated before my eyes, pulling me with a force that combined envy and curiosity. I found myself mulling over reasons why it was OK to invade Vito's privacy. I told myself it was only natural and right for me to be as intimate with Vito as I could be, to know him as well as I could, even if it meant peeking into private parts of his past. And then I thought to myself, "he doesn't have to know." There it was. My whole life was one big secret, and now I was going to intentionally drag another skeleton into my closet.

I went back downstairs. I went back to the liquor cabinet. I went back to the bottle of Old Crow. I poured myself four more fingers. Once again, I didn't bother with any ice. I drank it down.

And then, within moments, I was back upstairs, pulling the rubber band off the bundle of blank envelopes, pulling the sheets of paper out of the one labeled June 18, 1942, and then I began to read.

June 18, 1942

Dear Frederick,

Yippee, I'm a sailor! My new mate Tommy and I went to a cheap photo studio here at the base to get our picture taken. Enclosed you will find one fancy snapshot of me rigged out in my dress whites complete with a Dixie Cup hat. I look pretty crackerjack, don't I? Technically I can't say exactly where the base is, but I will say it's a place you've heard of … a place where there's a girl named Tootsie who plays the ukulele and wears a grass skirt and swivels her hips.

When I first checked into boot camp at the Great Lakes Naval Training Station in March, I got my shots, I got my buzz cut, and I threw away my civvies. I was lucky enough to get a uniform that actually fit me. Most of the guys had to find someone to alter their outfits. Seeing how you sew so well, you'd have been a big hit back there.

I got my sea bag with my name stenciled on the side and learned how to roll all my clothes and gear inside it according to strict regulations. We each got a hammock, a mattress, and two mattress covers, which Tommy calls 'fart sacks,' one pillow, two pillow covers and two cream-colored, woolen blankets. We're supposed to roll all this bedding together with our clothes into a bundle and stuff it inside our sea bag, which we then have to sling around our shoulders while we're marching around with happy smiles on our faces. It's a lot of weight to carry. I don't think any of us like that part.

I managed to make it through basic training without punching out Chief Petty Officer Riley— even though I swear the guy was asking for it every day. Riley is the type of guy who gets his jollies from all of it: marching, calisthenics, scrubbing clothes, rifle-over-your head drills, pulling oars in a boat. You name it. I guess he whipped us into shape, because by the end, whenever Riley said 'jump,' we jumped.

After I finished boot camp, I shipped out to my current location to start training to be a sonarman. Already I'm better than a bat at sending out sounds to detect my prey, so watch out! Ping! When I completed my course I was promoted to sonarman third class. Tomorrow I'm going to deploy on my new boat. The censor won't let me say the name of the boat. But I think I can say it's the kind of boat that goes under the water. Once I'm on the boat, I'll get my own locker, so I won't have to carry this damn sea bag around on my shoulder any more. According to Riley, that's how I'll know I'm a full-fledged sailor.

I like the idea of being in a boat that goes under the water. My first time on a boat was on a boat that was on top of the water. I puked my guts out. Do you know the words 'pitch' and 'yaw?' The damn thing pitched and yawed and bobbled up and down on the rough seas like a yo-yo that was trying out all the tricks from 'hop the fence' to 'around the world.' Half of us were hanging our heads over the side spewing like fountains. Tommy says I'll get used to it, so get over it. I'm hoping that the underwater version of the boat will be less bobbling.

I know the last time we talked things were pretty rough. I admire your guts for doing what you did. But I still don't think it was the right thing to do. The way I look at it, you're an actor. You could've just acted like a regular Joe and kept quiet about your private life. Meanwhile, the damn Nazis and Japs are trying to take over the world. We need everyone to stop them. And what exactly are you going to do now, get a job in one of the factories?

Believe it or not, despite everything, I slightly miss you. I won't get any more gooey than that.

Your pal,

Vito

I WENT BACK TO THE ENVELOPE AND SHOOK IT, JUST IN case I'd missed the photograph of Vito and Tommy in their dress whites. But clearly Vito had mailed the picture to Freddy and didn't have a copy to keep for himself. That was a disappointment. I'd have given anything to see a photo of Vito in his sailor uniform.

But who the hell was Tommy? Now I had a new pal of Vito's that I could stew about.

Next I pulled up the first letter from Freddy to Vito care of Pearl Harbor Naval Base, which was dated July 20, 1942, to see what Freddy made of Vito's letter.

July 20, 1942

Dear Vito,

Actually, Vito, I am doing my bit to stop the world from going to hell. I dropped out of school and got a job at the Galvin Manufacturing plant on West Harrison Street where we make a little number called a walkie talkie so you hot shots in the military can yack back and forth to each other about how brave you are even when you're up to a mile apart.

Nice picture! Tommy's quite a cute kid. That uniform fits him pretty tight. I suppose you just have to snap your fingers and Tommy takes care of you the way you like to be taken care of—though rumor has it there are 13 buttons standing in his way. Who the hell came up with that? What do you do when you gotta pee really bad? I suppose they wanted you sailor boys to stay buttoned up as much as possible.

After work yesterday I dropped by our favorite Loop giggle room, where I met an older gentleman named Clarence who, following a few beers, proceeded to tell me how back in his day he used to go to a hole in the wall joint on Tooker Alley called the Dil Pickle Club, spelled with just one 'l' in the Dil, as he insisted on pointing out. Let's just say it sounded like it was my kind of joint. Clarence said there was a sign on the door that read "Step High, Stoop Low and Leave Your Dignity Outside." Unfortunately the club closed in '36, but it sounds like it was the place to be back in the day, and looking at him now I suspect back then Clarence was a top pick for his fellow travelers.

Despite the difference in our ages, Clarence tried to make some advances in my direction, but I told him I was already taken. Is that still true? I don't really know any more since I'm starting to feel like it's going to be many a moon before I see you again. Unfortunately, Clarence was about the only thing going on at our favorite club. As far as I can tell, since the War started all the prime beef has joined up with Uncle Sam in one way or another.

My new friend Minnie says the situation is even worse with regard to her special female friends. She refers to them as the kind of women who drink beer from the bottle. The Armed Forces apparently gobbled them all up, too. Minnie says she would have signed up herself, but she claims she's got flat feet, whatever that means. Maybe it's a secret code for something. She and I have been gassing it up on the weekends at Benny the Bum's, a bar on Clark Street that's popular with soldiers and sailors and, uh, men of a certain sort. It's a little cheesy. Let's just say it's not the kind of place to wear your good clothes. Minnie and I are practically a couple. It's fun to go out together and keep 'em guessing!

By the way, Minnie is a singer and a piano player. She's also an actress, surprise, surprise, and we're thinking of getting together with Carl to form a theater troupe. Oh yeah, Carl, like me, was deferred, only his deferral was for a respectable medical condition, which pissed him off since he, like you, was gung-ho to get out there and mix it up with the Nazis. In his case, it's personal, him being Jewish.

Minnie and I sometimes drag him out with us to Benny the Bum's. But, as you can imagine, Carl just sits there drinking and smoking his pipe in his vaguely intellectual way, listening to the music, and he won't even consider talking to a stranger, be it a man or a woman. Phooey.

On some weekends the loop fills up with sailors who, I guess, are coming down from Great Lakes Naval Base. Seafood everywhere! But, not a drop to drink for this parched boy. And, of course, no Vito. Will you ever get shore leave? I know you can't say where you and your boat are and all that, but, gosh, you must get some time off for good behavior. Or maybe your behavior isn't so good, knowing you.

When you said you slightly missed me I just about

creamed my corn. I guess I can say the same. I sort of miss you, too.

Your degenerated pal,
    Frederica

As soon as I finished reading Freddy's letter, I put my hand over the remaining pile of blank envelopes that contained the letters written by Vito back to Freddy. I thought by covering them with my hand, maybe I could pause long enough to find the resolve to stop what I was doing. I knew I was snooping. I was slinking further and further down a path that would never allow me to turn back. But what could I do? I couldn't unread what I'd read or quash my jealousy by stopping now. Whatever inhibition I ought to have felt had evaporated as soon as I'd swallowed the Old Crow.

Freddy had been pretty flamboyant in his letter, and I could only imagine how anxious Vito must have been about that. Freddy didn't seem to care that the censors or even one of Vito's fellow sailors might find and read the letter. He at least had the good sense to sign it "Frederica." But the rest of the letter was pretty thinly veiled.

The fact that Vito still had the letter after all these years meant he'd had to stash it somewhere in his sea bag in order to hold on to it. That alone told me his feelings for Freddy were strong enough to overcome the risk of having someone stumble onto his private letters and put two and two together.

But it wasn't another sailor who had stumbled onto the letter. It was me.

15

I lifted my hand off the pile of Vito's letters and placed it on my forehead. I thought about getting another slug of Old Crow. But then I started thinking about how it would look to Vito when he came home. How was I going to explain being drunk as a skunk on a Monday night?

I decided I didn't need any more fortification. And what difference would it make if I had one more drink? I was going to keep going until I'd read all the letters and I knew it. I picked up the next envelope in the pile and shook it until Vito's next letter fell out.

September 7, 1942

My dear Frederica,

You're a naughty girl to write misleading innuendo and make degenerate jokes about me and my buddy Tommy. What kind of girlfriend are you? And when you write about yourself, please don't play games with gender. I know it's a gag to you, but it confuses everyone. The next time you write, be sure to let me know that you get what I'm telling you. Remember the military has privates but no privacy— and absolutely no sense of humor.

I'm glad to hear you got a good job. We don't use walkie talkies on my kind of ship, but I know a lot of sailors and soldiers use them. It's good to know you're doing something you're proud of.

And I'm glad you have a new pal to hang out with. Minnie sounds like a lot of fun. I'm not surprised to hear about Carl still being a stick in the mud. It's too bad he didn't qualify to enlist, because I'm pretty sure he's got relatives in Europe that are in hot water. We're gonna stop 'em. We've got to!

On my side of the world it's the Japs who seem to think they're the master race. Where do these people come up with this bs? Sometimes I can't believe the world we live in. You'd think people could just learn to get along, to live and let live.

Now about those thirteen buttons. One guy here said it has to do with the 13 original colonies. But that's bunk. It's just part of the discipline. The Navy is serious about discipline with respect to everything we do. Yes, sir. No, sir. Right away, sir. Whatever you want, sir! They regulate the hatches on the boats, so why not on the uniforms, too?

By now all of us sailors have learned how to work within the regulations. For example, if for some reason an alarm sounds, the hatches get closed quicker than you'd ever imagine. Also, most of us know how to dress in the dark. Tommy's got a technique all his own that has to do with how he lays out his gear, which he keeps in an arrangement between his mattress and his mattress cover. He says everything stays put so he can reach under the mattress cover and retrieve any article he needs even without looking.

A lot of guys reach for things in the dark on a ship at night. It's pretty eerie, to tell you the truth. Because everything and everyone has learned how to run silent, especially on my kind of boat. I've learned that some kinds of silence are pretty loud. I just keep thinking how all around me I'm surrounded by seamen. Ha. Ha.

Speaking of which, I'm learning more and more about how to do my job, which, as you know, does involve my ears quite a bit. It's a lot like table tennis: ping and pong. Of course what you want is a lot of ping and not so much pong. And that's how it's been for me so far. So don't worry.

But don't hold your breath when it comes to seeing me in your neck of the woods. If I get shore leave anytime soon it's gonna be on base or on a distant shore. Maybe at Christmas they'll cut us a break and let us go home. But somehow I think the Emperor of Japan is gonna nix that. We'll see.

I've enclosed another snapshot that Tommy took of me. This one shows off my biceps. Not bad, eh? That's from way more pushups than any sane man would do! All the sailors here are starting to look like muscle men because what else is there to do on a boat besides swabbing the deck and calisthenics? Unfortunately when I say "swabbing the deck" I'm not talking in code.

Your pal,

Vito

December 24, 1942

Dear Vito,

OK, I get it. Seeing as how it's almost Christmas I'll be a good girl and only write nice things!

Ha. Ha. Just kidding!

So, yes, now that you mention the code thing, I must say I miss you swabbing the deck. It's one of your best talents, baby! I haven't been doing any calisthenics, but I have been keeping in shape in my own way. I follow the rationing diet. Everything tasty is rationed, so I just don't eat. You think I'm joking? I keep my eye out for seafood, but even that has been in short supply.

Minnie says skinny boys can eat all they want and never gain a pound. She herself says she has no such luck and it's made worse because she has a particular passion for pound cake. Luckily for her, the government is talking about rationing butter now that it's getting so scarce. I told her she'll be on the rationing diet before she knows it.

Not that she needs to lose weight. She has a great figure and she's plenty skilled when it comes to figuring how to use it!

As for me, I'm still making walkie talkies at the factory. But at work I have no one to walkie and talkie with. Well, no men, anyway. There are plenty of women here at the factory. And then on my own time it's mostly me and Minnie. I did run into Clarence again recently at our favorite club. He said as far as he can see it's getting to be slim pickings when it comes to eligible men among the civilian population. All the available men are either old or disabled or ???

Oh, wait! It's the ??? part that we care about, isn't it? Only some of the ??? men joined up anyway. And now you can't say anything to them because someone's always looking over their shoulder. Have I got all that right?

You'll have to let me know if my way of putting things is sufficiently discreet for your liking. I should think a sailor's sea bag would be a private sanctuary.

But maybe not. In fact, the more I think about how men are, the more I think you're right to be careful.

I can certainly picture all you sailors lying in the dark in your hammocks. Such a lot of swaying, I imagine. Or have you learned how to do whatever you do without swaying? I guess it's not so much of a side to side movement as an up and down one. I've been doing a lot of that myself, as you can imagine. Speaking of which, I loved your biceps snapshot. Please send more photographs. I have a lot of up-and-down work to do and nothing does the trick for me quite the way your snapshots do. Minnie warns me I'm gonna get a bad case of acne if I keep it up. But that's just an old wive's tale. My skin is as pure as the new fallen snow, which we've been getting quite a lot of this year.

It's Christmas eve and the snow has put me in a Christmas mood. Roosevelt said in his speech tonight that all the defense-related plants will be closed tomorrow for the first time since the war began. Minnie and I are gonna get together at her place. She's making a turkey dinner with all the trimmings. We'll even have pound cake and ice cream!

I only wish it was like the last world war, when everyone took a break from fighting for Christmas. I keep thinking about you and the ping pong, and sometimes I get nightmares when I start hearing pongs. My biggest fear is that I suddenly won't hear back from you anymore. Promise me that even if you're mad at me you'll still drop me a line to let me know you're OK.

I'm sorry it's taken me so long to write. For one thing, I didn't get your last letter, which you dated September 7th until the first week of November. I guess the pony express isn't running as fast as it used to. I hope you get this, wherever you are, before spring—that is, if you can even tell whether or not it's spring in whatever part of the world you're in.

I hope when you get shore leave you aren't too distracted by all the girls in hula skirts and remember your old flame who waits for you by the fireside (well … by the space heater, anyway) at home!

With sincere affection
Your darling Frederica

February 14th 1943

Dear Frederica,

It's Valentine's Day and right now every sailor on board is stretched out in his hammock writing a letter to his sweetheart. So here I am writing to you— yes, you! But maybe I shouldn't be. You weren't very good at following my directions in your last letter. You've got to tone down the screwy jokes, baby. My nerves are already on edge from the ping pong. Now

I think, suppose some wayward sea dog has it in for me and decides to rummage through my sea bag. It's no gag. Any one of the animals on this boat would see right through your nutty jokes if he read one of your letters.

That's especially true in this crazy scene we're in. None of us boys has a normal outlet for our biological needs. We're all hot to trot but there's no easy way to trot in this situation. Certain guys seem to be having thoughts about fooling around in ways that they wouldn't normally have contemplated. But you can't tell what angle any particular guy is coming from. Abstinence is the official line. Maybe I'm just cynical, but I don't think that's the way everyone is handling it. Of course, whenever we get shore leave and get back to the base, all bets are off.

It's amazing to realize how much people communicate with their eyes. I was in the library on base the other day and I realized it wasn't a book the man across from me was reading, it was me!

After living with the same group of guys for months on end you get to the point where everyone knows everything about everyone else. And I mean everything. We have sailors from all over the U.S. here. They come from all walks of life, all religions, and even all races (no Japs, of course). And most of us don't care about each other's differences. But there are some who do. There's a petty officer in the unit who, to put it kindly, really is petty.

My pal Tommy, for example, knows plenty about me. He knows about my preferences when it comes to certain things. He's not the same religion as you and me, but does he care? No. And that's why I like him. I trusted my gut in telling him all about it one night and I'm glad I did. I really needed a sidekick I could talk to.

His girlfriend Doris writes to him once a week. I'm only mentioning that because getting mail is about the biggest kick we get around here. I look forward to the days when Tommy gets a letter from Doris almost as much as he does. Of course, he reads them to me and I soak it all up. I haven't read him any of your letters. But maybe I will at some point. We'll see. It would help if you wrote something nice and clean.

As far as the war goes, I can't wait for it to be over. To be honest, we had a pretty close call the other day with the Japanese navy. I can't say much about it, except to say that it was the kind of thing that puts everything else in perspective. When our lives are on the line we're all one team here. No one cares about politics or religion or anything else. Sometimes I can persuade myself that whatever differences there are between us don't matter. They really don't. We all want the same things. For the life of me I don't see why the enemy doesn't get that. They started this whole mess. And for what? How is it possibly going to end well for them, no matter what happens?

If I get out of this alive, I'm going to dedicate myself to my work. You should see the night sky here, F. Without saying where I am, I can tell you it's a place where there's no ambient light to dilute the view of the heavens. Looking up at the stars is one of the few things that gets me out of my thoughts, because I realize how vast the universe is and how utterly silly war is. What a waste!

Some nights I have great views of Ursa Major, Ursa Minor, and, of course, now that it's winter, I can see my buddy Orion, whose belt and sword is crystal clear. What that means is: I'm still in the northern hemisphere. That covers a lot of ground so that's not giving much away. But it's that, the colossal scale of everything, that helps me put the war in its place.

The middle star in Orion's belt is actually not a star but a nebula, which is a massive stellar nursery. The mechanics of star formation fascinates me. I can't wait to get back to school and have a look at the nebula through the Yerkes telescope. Professor Arden says the Orion nebula has a noticeably greenish tint to it. At one time astronomers thought the color was due to an unknown element which they called nebulium. Later they discovered the color originates from doubly ionized oxygen that depends on the quiescent and collision-free environment found in the high vacuum of deep space.

I can't believe I just wrote that to you. I know your eyes are glazing over about now. But this is the stuff that gets me excited, and frankly it's where my mind goes when nothing else is going on. As a matter of fact, if you must know, my nickname here on the ship is Dr. Zarkov. You know who he is, right? He's the egghead from the Flash Gordon movies. It's fine with me. I'm happy fighting against Ming the Merciless.

Your pal
    Doc

I was surprised that Vito had given Freddy such a hard time about the innuendo in his letter when Vito's letter was hardly any more subtle. He'd written about guys having unusual thoughts about their biological needs and about some guy who'd given him the once over in the base library. I guess Vito figured he could explain these things to the censors and defend anything he'd written if he'd been called out because his implication was that whatever weird behavior was going on was coming from other guys and not from himself.

He was right about all the sexual tension in the air during the war. I remember it in my army platoon, too. I was surrounded by a bunch of frisky soldiers, and we were in a situation that was sometimes so dangerous that we felt like we had nothing to lose. I was too timid to do anything about it, but boy did I feel it.

Vito was also right when he told Freddy that getting letters was a big deal. The only letters I ever got were from my mother. They were nice and all. But I was jealous of the guys who had adoring girlfriends, or good pals, or anyone besides their mother who'd take the time to write to them.

And then there was all that stuff Vito wrote about the Orion nebula. My first thought after I finished reading it was, how am I going to stop myself from calling him 'Dr. Zarkov?' To me it was an even better nickname for him than 'Vito Finito,' which was his nickname in the boxing ring. The two nicknames said a lot about Vito. I loved both parts of him. The Finito part got to one part of my anatomy and the Zarkov part got to another, but it was the Zarkov side of him that I most trusted. Vito's boxing character was a double-crosser, a two-timer when you got right down to it. And I knew that if a guy would throw a fight, he'd throw over a lover just as easily.

I also knew that Vito had thrown over a lover once before. He'd thrown over Freddy some time during the war. I wanted to know why. And I wanted to make sure I didn't end up in the same situation.

16

———

As I sat on the bed obsessing about Vito's letter to Freddy, I heard a noise from downstairs. Someone had opened the front door. It had to be Vito. He must have come home early from the gym. And there I was, up in the bedroom, surrounded by his old letters. The moment he came upstairs he was going to see that I was snooping. And I was tipsy. I had to do something. And I knew I had to do it fast.

I stuffed all the letters and envelopes back into the letter box. I didn't have time to put the rubber bands back around the bundles or put them in any kind of order. I crammed everything back in the box helter-skelter. I took the box to the closet and lobbed it onto the back of the top shelf. I picked up the pile of Vito's workout clothes that I'd left on the floor and tossed them on the shelf in front of the box. I stepped out of the closet and closed the closet door.

I heard Vito call my name from downstairs. I could tell he was in the kitchen. I knew he wondered where I was. I couldn't think of a good reason to be in the bedroom. Nor was there any good reason for me to be drunk on a work night. I was in a panic. I didn't know what to do.

Then I had an idea that seemed screwy at first. But I couldn't think of anything else. And then I thought maybe it wasn't so crazy. I scurried out of the bedroom and headed across the hall to the bathroom. I turned on the shower and peeled off my clothes, almost tripping over myself as I got out of my pants. And then, holding my breath, I stepped into the shower while the water was still cold. I had to struggle to keep quiet from the shock of the cold water.

Within moments Vito was upstairs, knocking on the bathroom door. He called through the door, "I'm home. Are you in there?"

With the water still running, I stepped out of the shower, covered myself with a towel and opened the door. I was dripping wet, but I'd sobered up enough to put an expression on my face that I hoped was the picture of innocence. My expression changed when I saw him. The right side of his face was swollen.

"I had a crack-up at the gym," he said. "You know that kid I've been coaching?"

I nodded.

"I was showing him some moves. While we were sparring, he threw a punch that caught me by surprise."

"Are you OK?" I reached up and gently touched his face.

He grimaced. "Yeah, I'm OK, but don't touch it." He looked at me then as if he was just taking in the situation. "You're all wet."

"Yeah, I … I was reading and I fell asleep. I was taking a shower to wake up."

"Oh yeah?" He stared at me. I saw his eyes travel down my torso. "How awake are you?"

I immediately felt self-conscious. He was staring at my towel, or more precisely, at my crotch. "Uh, what you're looking at is shrunken from the cold water."

"Oh is it? Well maybe I can do something about that."

The moment he spoke, I began unshrinking. "So do you … want to do something about it right now?" I asked, trying to sound innocent.

"I do," he said. He lifted his arm and sniffed under it, while keeping his eyes fixed on me. "As a matter of fact, I need to take a shower, too. Maybe I should join you."

He began unbuttoning his shirt. In a moment he'd taken it off and dropped it. Then he unbuckled his belt, let his pants fall to the floor, and stepped out of them. Now he was wearing only his underwear. His chest, shoulders and biceps were on full display. It was a sight that never failed to arouse me. My desire became visible as my growing erection started to push against my towel. That caught his eye.

"It looks like your towel is getting in the way of something," he said. As he spoke there was a movement in the crotch of his underwear that echoed what was happening with me.

He reached out and gingerly pulled off my towel—and there I was, standing at full mast. "I can definitely do something about that!" he said. He dropped to his knees.

"Wait a minute." I put my hands on the top of his head. "What about your face? I thought you didn't want anything to touch it."

"Don't worry," he said. "I'm a pro. I can take any amount of pain." He was on his knees staring right at me. "You are *so* damn pretty." He darted out his tongue, licking me on the tip.

Within minutes my mood had skipped from panic to embarrassment to full-on longing. I forgot about the letters and my snooping and Freddy and Tommy and the war. I let myself slide all the way deep into his mouth.

After several minutes he got me so worked up I was almost ready to cum. I was about to tell him how close I was, when he spun me around to face the other way. "Bend over," he said, "Grab the sink." I did. He said, "Now I'm gonna help you wake up even more." He stood. I turned to look back at him. He was hard, rock solid, already moist at the tip.

"Jesus, Vito."

He used his hands to spread my cheeks and then slowly and gently he began to push inside me.

My voice broke. "Oh, Vito. Vito!" I was opening up easily. I wanted him so much.

And there we were. Suddenly we were everything we ever wanted to be. We were naked in our bathroom, joined together as one. The water in the shower had become very hot. Steam billowed from the bathtub. Beads of water dripped off my skin from the steam, but also from sweat trickling off my forehead, from under my arms, from my chest, and from my abdomen. Vito pushed in and out of me, slowly at first, in a steady, sensual rhythm. He wrapped his hands around my chest and brushed the tips of my nipples with his fingers. He gently called my name. He nibbled on my ear. He murmured, cooing, "Oh Elliot," drawing out the vowels in my name. "I love you. I love you."

I wished I had never doubted him. I felt the pounding force of his erection as he thrust in and out with growing urgency. In that moment, I could feel how much he loved me, how much he wanted me. It was everything I'd dreamed about. I swore to myself that I'd never let myself feel jealous again.

I thrust back against him as he drove into me. And then Vito cried out "Wait!" He stopped moving. He grabbed me hard around the waist. He moaned in a sound that went from a low growl to a high pitch. And then with an unstoppable tremor he began to spurt deep inside me, while he called my name. "Elliot, Elliot!"

When he shouted my name I, too, began to spurt. It gushed from me all over the bathroom floor. Then the spasming of our bodies slowed in a long decrescendo until we were just lightly pressed together. And at the end I felt between us just the barest tremor.

We were one.

17

I was flying high when I got to the office the next day. I felt like a new man down to my bones. I beamed at everyone I saw, from the conductor on the train, to the pretty woman who ran the cigar stand in the building lobby, to the earnest elevator operator who'd memorized my floor. They were all beautiful. Peggy had a new hairdo. I oohed and ahhed until she said, "Go on, Mr. Blake, you're gonna make me blush."

There was a note on my desk. It said Miss Minnie McNally had called and would I please telephone her back at my earliest convenience. After that, Peggy had written a telephone number. I picked up the message and stepped back over to Peggy's desk outside my office. "When did this come in?" I handed her the note.

"Oh yes, Miss McNally. She called just before you got in this morning. I told her you'd be here by nine and she said, 'Please have him telephone me when he gets in.'"

"Thanks, Peggy."

I went back into my office and closed the door. I had just seen Minnie at the funeral on Sunday afternoon. I'd been preoccupied with Vito and Freddy, but I did remember that she'd walked in with the other members of *The Shadow's Voice* cast and crew. She hadn't said a word to me.

I dialed the number she'd given Peggy. The woman who answered said "WGN, how may I direct your call?" I gave her Miss McNally's name and the woman said, "Oh, you want Minnie? Hold on a minute." Then I heard some background chatter and after a moment, Minnie came on the line.

"Mr. Blake," she said. "Thank you for calling me back. There's something I want to talk to you about. But I can't right now. I'm at work at the moment."

"At work?"

"Yes. On the WGN switchboard."

"The switchboard?" I was confused. "What happened? Did you lose your radio job?"

"No, no. I'm still on the show," she said. "This switchboard engagement is what we in the trade call a day job. On *The Shadow's Voice* I don't make the kind of money the big shots make."

I'd never thought about what a radio job paid. Minnie was good at her job. In fact, over the years I'd been listening, I thought she was the best character on the show. "That hardly seems fair," I said.

"Yeah, well that's showbiz. Anyway, I've got a couple of side gigs to add a few bucks to the McNally household fund."

"I see."

"I can't talk to you now." She paused. I heard her suck in her breath. She'd been speaking to me using the voice of a professional telephone operator. But now the tone of her voice changed. She seemed nervous. "I wanted to talk to you," she said. "I'd like to make a date for later. Are you free tonight?"

"A date?" I was surprised.

"I don't mean a going out kind of date. Sorry. I should've been more clear. I just want to meet to talk." She lowered her voice. "But it's about something private. It has to do with Leonard Lehnert."

"Oh," I said. That made it part of my job. "Of course," I said. I picked up my pencil to write down an address. "Where do you want to meet?"

"I thought maybe you could visit me at my other side job. I play piano and sing at a bar off the lobby of the Hotel Sherman downtown called the Dome Room. My piano gig is on Tuesday and Friday nights. Could you drop by the Dome Room tonight for a drink?"

"Tonight?"

"Unless you're a teetotaler or something."

"I'm not."

"OK. good. It's at the Hotel Sherman. It's on Randolph Street. You know it?"

"I've heard of it." I said. "What time should I come?"

"I start my first half-hour set at seven. Then I go on a break before I start again. To tell you the truth, there usually aren't too many people in the bar at that hour. Just my die-hard fans. The crowd picks up after nine. So I could talk to you at 7:30, after my first set."

"How about if I come at seven? That way I can hear you perform before we talk."

"Sure. Why not? I'm not bashful. We'll talk when I'm done."

"All right," I said. "I'll be at the Dome Room at seven."

THE HOTEL SHERMAN WAS AT THE WEST END OF Randolph in the theater district downtown. The hotel had a reputation for being one of the nicer hotels in town. I'd never been to the Dome Room, though I'd heard all about it from my buddy Maurice. Maurice called it the "Do Me Room." He said the place was a favorite hangout for certain men, men who could blend in at a place that anyone might happen to go to. It was perfect for a guy like Maurice, who didn't want to take a chance on getting caught in a raid at one of the strictly all-male bars. Having just read Freddy's letters, I knew Minnie was no stranger to men like Maurice. I wondered if she'd ever met him.

I got to the 'Do Me Room' at five minutes to seven. I sat down at the bar and looked around. I didn't expect Maurice to be there, and he wasn't. I knew he rarely went out before ten p.m. But I was glad I wouldn't have to explain to him what I was doing. Strictly speaking, I was working. But I'd be lying if I didn't admit that I was also eyeballing the men in the bar in a way that went beyond just looking for Maurice. There was one particularly good-looking fellow who was sitting about five stools down from me. He was eyeballing me, too.

The bar had a modern design with sweeping curves. It meandered across one side of the room and was lined with elegant square-cushioned stools. A stage behind the bar had a cupola dome of its own. On the stage was a piano. Minnie stood beside it, shuffling through a stack of sheet music. She wore a white tuxedo with a white shirt, a white tie, and a white top hat. The white in her outfit was offset by bright red lipstick and red patent leather high heels. Before she could even sit down, the man who'd given me the once-over called out, "Hey, Minnie. Play 'It's Almost Like Being in Love.'"

I knew that song. It was from the musical *Brigadoon*, which was playing on Broadway. It didn't surprise me that show tunes were part of Minnie's repertoire.

Minnie called back to the bar patron, "What happened, George? Did you almost fall in love?"

George looked around the room. "You know it, Minnie. Every night!" Then, to my surprise, he turned and looked directly at me. He lifted his cocktail glass and nodded. "Especially tonight," he said.

Minnie looked at where George was looking and saw me. She nodded at me, too. "I'm sorry, George," she said. "That one's a friend of mine and he's taken."

"By who?"

"Why, by me, sweetheart. Who'd you think?"

"I thought you liked girls, Minnie."

"Oh, I do," said Minnie. "I like everybody. Even you, sweetie." Then she sat down and started to play and sing "Almost like Being in Love."

The exchange between Minnie and George astonished me. First, I was amazed by how openly flirtatious George was. Second, I was abashed that Minnie seemed to know I was already taken. She said I was taken by her. But I think she was covering for me. I had the feeling she knew more about me than she could have learned from our brief encounters at the studio and the funeral. I knew she'd been friends with Freddy during the war. Since they worked together at *The Shadow's Voice*, I figured they must still be friends. And, of course, Freddy knew all about Vito.

In her first thirty minute set, Minnie sang three show tunes, two old-time ballads, and four contemporary top hits. All of the songs were by request, including two more requests by George. His last request was for the Judy Garland song, "Somewhere Over the Rainbow." During the final chorus, the part where 'birds fly over the rainbow' and 'why then, oh why can't I?,' Minnie called on everyone in the room to sing with her, which we did. After that Minnie stood up and called out, "OK, children, get out there and fly!" Then she climbed down from the stage, went to one of the small tables in the center of the room and waved me over.

"Thanks for coming," she said as we sat down. "How'd you like the set?" She took off her top hat, set it on the table, then shook out her hair, which was decidedly red.

"You are *good*," I said. "You're really good." I meant it, too. In fact, I was stage-struck. I felt shy when talking to someone with so much talent. I looked around the room. "You have a lot of fans here."

"Oh, yeah. Most of these boys and I go way back. I've had this gig for two years. At this point they all think I'm their mother hen."

"You've got a lot of stage presence. It comes out in the radio show, too."

"Thanks! What can I say? I'm a ham."

"Let me buy you a drink," I offered.

"I could go for a scotch on the rocks," she said. "How about you?"

"Scotch is good."

Minnie raised her hand and caught the bartender's eye. "Two of the usual, Walt." Then she turned to me. "Thanks for the offer, but you don't need to buy. I get free drinks every night as part of my gig. That's what the owner gives me in lieu of decent pay. I also have a tip bowl on the bar that usually does pretty well."

"I saw the bowl," I said. "And I noticed that everyone who requested a song dropped coins in the bowl."

Minnie nodded. "Once in a while, I even get a bill. Usually it's at the end of the set and usually it's for 'Over the Rainbow,' like George did tonight. The boys can't seem to get enough of that."

Walt arrived with our drinks and set them in front of us. Walt was an older gentleman, whose crisp black jacket, white shirt, black tie, and urbane manner gave him an air of elegance. Earlier I'd watched him mix drinks in an offhand way, as though he knew every cocktail in the book … and plenty more that weren't.

I glanced up at Walt but spoke to Minnie. "You're better than Judy Garland, if you ask me."

"Why, Mr. Blake!" She lifted her glass and I lifted mine. We clinked them together and each took a sip. She said, "I think I'm gonna like you more than I knew."

I blushed. I really was stage-struck. "I … I hope so."

Walt heard what I said about Minnie being better than Judy Garland. "He's right, you know," he said to her. "You are better. I've always said so."

"So, listen." Minnie paused, waiting until Walt left. She looked around, then lowered her voice. "The reason I asked you here is to talk about Leonard. But first I want to give you some background."

"OK."

"I'm going to start with Freddy. You know him, right? Freddy Foster from the show?"

"Yes."

"Well, Freddy and I go way back—even further back than I go with these boys here at the Dome Room."

"OK."

"And the thing is ... I know a lot about Freddy, including all about his romances from the past. So, well ..." She stared at me now, looking straight into my eyes. Her eyes were large, and looked even larger due to the eyeliner and mascara she wore. "Well ...." She looked around. "You can see what kind of a place this is. As you might imagine, working here I get to know what's what. Anyway ..." She took her hand off her scotch and put it on my wrist. "Not to beat around the bush ... I know all about the relationship Freddy had with your friend Vito. And so I figure I know what that means about you, too. You get me?"

I blushed again, even though what she was saying was hardly a surprise. I nodded.

"So you see," she continued. "I knew what was up the minute I saw you and Vito come in together at the funeral. I never knew Vito personally. Before the funeral, we'd never actually met in person. But I knew of him on account of various pictures that Freddy has of Vito from before the war ... when he and Vito were friends."

"I see."

"And after overhearing that little spat between

Freddy and Vito at the funeral, I figure you must have put two and two together, too. I mean, about Vito and Freddy. What I'm trying to say is … I have a pretty good idea about you and Vito being in the same kind of relationship that Freddy and Vito used to be in before they split up." She paused. "Am I right?"

I nodded.

"Good." She blinked and squeezed my wrist. "That's good." She took her hand from my wrist and put it back on her glass. She lifted her glass and took a swallow. She continued, "Under the circumstances, then, it might not surprise you to learn that along with knowing all about Freddy and Vito and, uh, you, I also happen to know that Leonard Lehnert was in the same boat."

"What?"

"Sorry. I shouldn't have put it that way … given what happened. What I mean is, Leonard was that way, too. I mean like the rest of you boys."

"But Leonard was married."

"Oh, angel!" She smiled. "Of course he was married. But Gloria knew all about it. She knew all about it from even before she and Leonard got married. They had a little arrangement, you see. It worked well for them … professionally and socially."

"Like at *The Shadow's Voice*."

"Yeah. Like there … and in general in our little social circle. The thing is, most of our friends are a bit funny—one way or another." Just then the bartender arrived with a second round of scotches and set them on the table in front of us. "Thanks, Walt," Minnie said.

"Who's your new boyfriend?" Walt asked.

"Never you mind, angel," said Minnie. "Like I said, he's taken."

I looked at Walt, who was smiling at me. "I'm Elliot," I said.

"I'm Walt. Nice to meet you, Elliot." Walt raised his eyebrows and bowed slightly.

"Now be a nice boy, Walt, and scoot out of here," said Minnie. "And help yourself to a tip from me out of the bowl."

"See ya," said Walt, who winked at me and left.

"All the men here are so friendly," I said.

"Oh, they're friendly all right," said Minnie. "But they're a tough crowd to please. At any other piano bar I'd have to introduce the customers to the new show tunes when they come out. Here at the Dome half the men have already seen the shows on Broadway before I even know what they are. It keeps me on my toes."

"I guess it helps with your tips."

"I get the tips for singing. Walt, on the other hand …" She looked around to see that Walt was back behind the bar. "He gets tips for making every guy here feel like a matinee idol. You name it, he'll make it. And it doesn't hurt that, given his age, he looks like he might have been a matinee idol himself once upon a time. As a matter of fact, if you ever find yourself wanting out of the insurance racket, you could always get a job at a joint like this—looking the way you do."

"Thanks," I said. "It would probably be a lot of fun."

"More fun than peddling insurance?"

"Actually, I'm a claims investigator these days. It's more like being a detective than a salesman."

"Well, that's why I wanted to talk to you. I've got a tip for you which my good pal Gloria doesn't know about."

Minnie took a sip from her scotch glass.

I did the same. "How well do you know Gloria?" I asked.

"Well, I know her from the show, of course. She's one of the writers. But even outside of work we've been friends. I've been friends with her and Leonard for years. Except I usually never saw them together."

"Why's that?"

"That was all part of their arrangement. She had her little affairs and he had his—but they had a rule that they never talked about it to each other. That way she didn't know about any sidelines he might have, and he didn't know about hers. I guess they thought it made it easier for them. Though I always thought it was kind of silly."

I nodded. But I didn't think their arrangement was silly. It made perfect sense to me.

"Anyway," Minnie continued, "both Gloria and Leonard thought of me as a confidant. So they both talked about their sidelines with me. And it was part of everybody's understanding, that they were both talking to me about everything, including the sidelines, and that I could be counted on to be as neutral as Switzerland. I never said boo to Leonard about Gloria's extracurricular activities with … " She stopped. "Well, that part isn't important to what you need to know about. Let's just say Gloria has had a fling or two of her own. But what you need to know is about Leonard's fling, which was really more than a fling. In fact, it was a steady years-long relationship with a guy named Ray McDonald, who is a Chicago policeman."

"A policeman? I didn't know there were any policemen who were … uh … like that."

"Oh honey, fellows like you are everywhere. Believe me. Working here, I've seen all kinds, from sweet and tender accountants like George over there to big beefy cops like Ray."

"You mean he comes in here?"

"Not only does he come in here, he works here. He's one of the bouncers."

"You mean he's here?"

"Not at the moment. That's what I want to tell you about. You see Ray is on vacation. He left just after Leonard's accident."

"OK."

"But that's only part of it. The main thing I want to tell you about is a priest. Maybe you saw him. Father Whalen. He was at Leonard's funeral the other night."

"I did see him," I said. "And so did my friend Vito.

Vito knew Father Whalen from the war. He said Father Whalen was a chaplain on the naval base at Pearl Harbor."

"That's right. That's just what Ray told me. That's how Ray and Father Whalen first got connected."

"Was Ray at the funeral?"

"No. He wasn't."

"Really?" That surprised me, given the years-long relationship Minnie had described. "What happened? Did he and Leonard break up or something?"

"No. Not as far as I know."

"Well, then if they were as close as you say they were, why didn't Ray come to the funeral?"

"That's what I want to know, Mr. Detective. That's exactly what I want to know."

18

———————

Wh_en Minnie called me Mr. Detective, I knew I'd come a long way. As I sat listening to her, I felt as if I was investigating a claim the way Martin Zimmerman would have wanted me to. I was pursuing the leads. I was asking questions. I was following my hunches. But most of all, I was skeptical, in the same way Martin always was.

Just then, I looked up to see George, the accountant, walking toward our table. He wore a polka-dotted bow tie that was just as endearing as the smile on his face.

"Now, Minnie," George said. "I won't stand for it. You've got to introduce me to your new friend, or I'll never speak to you again."

Minnie sighed. "That's tempting, George." But then she laughed. "Just kidding." She gestured toward each of us with her hands as she introduced us. "George, may I present Elliot Blake. Mr. Blake, this is George Gordon, who is also known here at the Dome as Pearly, on account of he's always clutching…"

"Never mind about that, Minnie," George said, before she could finish. Then he turned to me and bowed his head slightly. "I noticed you earlier tonight, Mr. Blake." He reached out his hand. "Please call me George," he said.

I took his hand and shook it. "And you can call me Elliot."

"OK," Minnie said. "You've officially met. And now, Georgie boy, you need to go back to your stool, turn your radar back on, tune it up, and look for new incoming aircraft. Like I was trying to tell you earlier tonight, this one's not flying in your formation."

"Oh, dear," said George. "Not an enemy, I hope."

"No, darling," said Minnie. "An ally, I'm sure. But he's taken. And from the looks of the guy who's taken him, he's taken by a guy you wouldn't want sore at you."

"Oh? It's like that, is it?" George smiled pleasantly.

"He's a boxer," I said.

"How stimulating!" George smiled again. But there was clearly disappointment on his face.

"Yeah," Minnie said. "It's titillating, ain't it? Now bend over here for a minute, Pearly, so I can fix your shirt."

George bent over. Minnie reached into George's shirt pocket and pulled out a ring. It was a plain gold band, like a wedding ring. She handed it to him. "Here," she said. "Put your camouflage back on and go back to your post on stool six. Mr. Blake and I have business to discuss."

"OK, well …" He slid the ring onto his finger. "You can't blame a fellow for trying, right?" He touched my arm. "I must say, it was nice to meet you, Elliot."

"Nice to meet you, too," I said.

After he left, Minnie said. "He's a nice kid. And not bad looking. But the poor sap has lousy radar. He's forward when he ought to be careful. Not every guy who comes into this place is looking for the same thing. There've been times when George has tried to get chummy with the wrong guy. Once he got beat up in the men's room. Ray had to go in there and break it up."

"Is George really married?"

"He's married. But he's married to a woman like Gloria, who sees the advantage in having a pal instead of a lover. Mrs. Gordon sometimes comes here with George for drinks on Monday nights, which is Ladies' Night. I've met her. She makes everybody laugh. She and Pearly are like a comedy act when they get going. The management likes it when guys bring their wives in—especially if the husband actually sits with his wife. It keeps the population here from looking off-balance like it does tonight."

I looked around. The men were all dressed like businessmen. But there were only a handful of women in the bar. "I see what you mean," I said. "Did Gloria ever come here with Leonard?"

"No. It wasn't like that for them. They kept everything separate. Leonard wouldn't have been comfortable having Gloria and Ray in the same room. Like I told you, the feeling between him and Ray, it was serious. They weren't just casual friends."

"So how does Father Whalen fit into this? How come he was at Leonard's funeral?"

"That's another thing I'm trying to figure out," Minnie said. "It surprised me."

"You said Father Whalen and Ray knew each other at Pearl Harbor. Maybe he knew Leonard, too."

"He did."

"Then why is it surprising he came to the funeral?"

"You haven't heard the whole story."

"Which is what?"

"It all started in Pearl Harbor, where Ray was stationed and Father Whalen was a chaplain. One day in the summer of 1942, Ray was caught in the act of … well, let's call it an indiscretion … which he was having with another sailor on the base."

"Caught by who? Another sailor?"

"No. They were caught by Father Whalen, who just happened to be in the same middle-of-nowhere, neck-of-the-woods spot where Ray and the other sailor met up. According to Ray, the spot was known to those in the know as a place where encounters like that might possibly happen."

"I see."

"After a disciplinary review, the other sailor was dishonorably discharged. But Ray was let off with a warning. It turned out that Father Whalen convinced the disciplinary board that, based on how he saw it, Ray was OK, just a regular guy who'd been hard up and made a mistake. He assured the board it was the other sailor who'd egged Ray into dishonorable behavior."

"So it sounds like Father Whalen did Ray a favor?"

"That's what Ray thought at first, too. But it turned out the reason he did Ray the favor was because the other sailor wouldn't go along with Father Whalen's demands. And, if I'm reading between the lines of what Ray told me correctly, it was also because Ray was even easier on the eyes than the other guy, and the way Father Whalen figured it, Ray was gonna become his new special friend, which Ray, unfortunately, was forced to do—because, well, he had no choice. Father Whalen told Ray he'd go back to the disciplinary board and change his tune if Ray didn't play ball. So for two months in the summer of '42 while Ray was at the base, he had to keep Father Whalen happy."

"Happy how?"

"Well, angel, Ray is very shapely—especially in the backside."

"Oh."

"All that was in the past. But then one night a few months ago, Father Whalen showed up here. He saw Ray and Leonard sitting at a table and right away he saw they were a couple. To be honest, they weren't very good at hiding it. Ray often put his arm around Leonard's shoulders in a 'he's my old buddy' kind of way. He thought nobody looking at them would think anything of it because Ray was a cop and the bouncer. It's all about what things you can and can't do in a place like this. Like, for example, you're never allowed to hold hands. Some nights it's a burlesque show in here, watching the creative ways guys have of touching while looking like a slap-happy baseball team."

"Did Ray talk to Father Whalen?"

"Ray never even saw him. First of all, Father Whalen wasn't wearing his clerical collar. He was dressed in a regular suit and tie, just like all these other men. He must have figured he'd have an easier time meeting a guy here if he was out of uniform. And then, too, once he spotted Ray he probably kept out of Ray's line of sight."

"So nothing happened?"

"No. Not with Ray. But Ray had to leave early that night to attend a big cop event at the Blackstone Hotel. Ray's police captain was retiring and Ray was invited to the retirement party. He had to keep up with things like that to stay on a good footing with his fellow cops."

"Did the other cops know he worked here?"

"Yeah. Some did. But you gotta remember, working here and coming here to meet people for illegal activities are two different things. Most people have no idea what's going on here at the Dome. This is a hotel bar. And the Sherman House is a respectable downtown hotel. Also, I know from the stories he told me that Ray pretended to be as straight as an arrow when he was on the force. He sometimes went so far as to make off-color jokes about sissies to divert any suspicion. I've seen guys cover up that way before. Even in this place, when Leonard wasn't here, Ray swaggered around the joint like he was John Wayne."

"Yeah," I said. "Some guys are like that." Vito had a way of swaggering that drove me wild.

"Of course, when he was here at the Dome, Ray sometimes would join in on the chorus of 'Somewhere Over the Rainbow'. So he wasn't pretending all the time."

Once again, I looked around. "It's nice to be in a place where you don't have to pretend."

"Ain't that the truth. Anyway, the point is: Father Whalen saw Ray that night, but Ray never saw Father Whalen. Otherwise he might have warned Leonard before he left for the retirement party at the Blackstone Hotel."

"What happened?"

"Once Ray left, Leonard was sitting by himself. Almost immediately Father Whalen went up to Leonard's table and sat down and started to chat with him. According to Leonard, Father Whalen talked from the get-go about how he'd noticed that Leonard had a boyfriend—like it was his way of making it clear he was just chatting with Leonard all friendly-like, and not flirting. He bought Leonard a couple of drinks. He went on chatting for a while. Gradually, he drew Leonard out, asking him questions about Ray, getting him to start talking about their relationship. Eventually, Leonard mentioned that Ray was a cop. Father Whalen asked Leonard if he had any pictures of the two of them."

"Seems like an odd thing to ask," I said.

"Leonard admitted to me that he was a bit soused by that point. And he was so proud of his relationship with Ray. He went into a hidden compartment in his wallet and took out a snapshot. It was a photo of Ray with his arms around Leonard, squeezing him tight. It was more than a buddy-buddy kind of photo. In fact, they were kissing. As soon as Father Whalen saw it, he snatched it off the table, stood up and stuck it in the inside pocket of his suit. Once he had the photograph, he turned on a dime. He gave Leonard a telephone number and instructed him to have Ray telephone him. He told Leonard he'd spill the beans to the cops about Ray's disciplinary hearing in Pearl Harbor, and then show them the photo, if Ray didn't call him within two days."

"Poor Leonard."

"It was bad for both of them—both Leonard and Ray."

"Did Ray call the guy?"

"What choice did he have? Before you know it, Ray

was back to being Father Whalen's special friend—keeping him happy just like he'd had to do in Hawaii."

"And what about Leonard?"

"All during this time, Ray and Leonard were still together. Leonard felt guilty. He blamed himself for showing Father Whalen the picture. Ray told him it wasn't his fault. How could he have known he was dealing with someone like that? Ray was always very sweet to Leonard."

"I can't imagine how terrible Leonard felt."

"He *did* feel terrible. And then something happened that made him feel worse." Minnie took a big slug of her whiskey. "Father Whalen had the photo of Ray and Leonard. But Father Whalen at that time didn't know who Leonard was, or where he lived, or anything about him. Then one day a few months ago, the *Tribune* ran an article about *The Shadow's Voice*. They included a publicity photograph of Leonard. Father Whalen saw the article and saw the photo."

"I know that photo," I interjected. "I have it in my case file."

Minnie nodded. "Well, after that, Whalen knew that Leonard was a big radio star—and he started right in again with the extortion routine. Apparently having Ray give him favors wasn't enough for him. He wanted more. This time he sent Leonard a letter in care of WGN, in which he threatened to mail the press the photo and tell the Tribune all about Leonard's secret life unless Leonard also agreed to give him sexual favors."

"So what happened?"

"Well, that's about as much as I know. Leonard got the extortion letter from Father Whalen two weeks ago. Ray told me all about it here at the Dome the next night. And the following weekend is when Leonard had his accident. The day after Leonard died, Ray came in and told us he was going away. He was devastated, obviously, by Leonard's death. He said he had two weeks vacation coming, that he didn't know what he was going to do, but that he wanted to go somewhere and be alone with his grief."

"I'm not sure I understand what you're saying? Do you think any of that has something to do with Leonard's death?"

"I don't know. I just know it makes me suspicious. I figured I should tell you. I thought, in your capacity, maybe you could find out if Father Whalen knows something. And maybe you can track down Ray. Nobody here who knows him has heard from him. I'm worried about him. It doesn't add up that he'd miss Leonard's funeral."

"I'm not sure how I could track down Ray. I don't even know what he looks like."

Minnie raised her finger. "Ah," she said. "I came prepared for that." She bent down under the table. Out of nowhere she produced a small purse. She popped it open and took out a photograph. "This is a picture

Pearly took of all of us on Ray's last night here." She showed me the photo. "That's Ray in the Hawaiian shirt. As far as I know, he's still in Chicago."

I studied the photo. "Can I keep this?"

"That's why I brought it. And, if you're willing, maybe you could track down Father Whalen at his church."

"Do you know which church it is?"

Minnie nodded. "Ray told me about it. It's called the Church of the Holy Family. It's on Roosevelt. It's somewhere on the west side. That's all I know."

"I'm not a Catholic," I said.

"Neither am I, darling," said Minnie.

"Vito is."

"That figures. Does he go to mass?"

"Not normally. He only goes on Christmas and Easter. According to him, he goes for reasons of nostalgia. It was a big deal to him when he was a kid."

"Ah. The sentimental type."

"He also likes opera. He's Italian."

Minnie laughed. "No kidding." She paused in thought, then said, "Say, maybe he can help you."

"I hope so. I've never even been inside a Catholic church."

"Me either," Minnie said. She hesitated a moment, as if she wanted to say something more, but wasn't sure about it. Finally, she said, "There's one more thing I need to tell you. When it comes to this spat between Freddy and Vito, I'm not Switzerland. I'm firmly on

Freddy's side of the fence. If you ask me, the way Vito treated Freddy during the war was all wrong."

"I don't know that much about it."

"Well, here it is in a nutshell. Like everyone else, Vito made Freddy feel bad for sitting out the war. I happen to think what Freddy did was brave. He refused to lie about himself. It wasn't his choice to sit out the war. It was the Army's choice. But instead of supporting Freddy, Vito got mad at him because he wouldn't pretend the way Vito did."

"You're saying Vito was sore because Freddy didn't enlist? That doesn't sound like Vito."

"Well, it wasn't mainly that. Mostly Vito was sore about Freddy's letters. Freddy wrote Vito letters during the war in which he was indiscreet about their relationship. Eventually, Vito's petty officer found the letters in Vito's personal belongings and Vito got into hot water."

"I didn't know."

"Vito was able to keep himself from being discharged or court-martialed, but he had to deal with the humiliation. Anyway, he blamed Freddy for what happened. He'd asked Freddy to tone down his letters. But I guess Freddy couldn't help himself. And then, after he got caught, Vito wouldn't forgive him."

I didn't want to put myself in between Vito and Minnie—or in between Vito and Freddy either, for that matter. So I tried to think of something nice to say about Freddy. I said, "Freddy's a talented guy. I hope he ends up taking the lead role in *The Shadow's Voice*. Overall, he's better than Roger. He's more expressive."

"I think so, too."

"To be honest, when I was thinking about who might benefit from Leonard's death, the only people I could think of were Gloria, Freddy and Roger. Gloria, because she's getting the insurance money, and Freddy and Roger because either of them might be able to step into the lead role."

"Well, you can forget about Freddy or Roger. Freddy is too much of a sweetheart to have had anything to do with it. And Roger is as bad as the cowardly lion. He didn't even have the courage to ask Carl for the lead. As for Gloria, you gotta understand that she really loved Leonard. What good would it do her to lose him? Money from an insurance claim can't make up for what she lost."

I realized I didn't know much about Leonard's relationships with his fellow actors. Since Leonard and Freddy shared a common interest in men, it made me wonder if they'd ever been interested in each other. "Were Freddy and Leonard friends?"

Minnie seemed to read my mind. "Yeah," she said, "but just regular friends. They were never together. Leonard only had eyes for Ray. And as for Freddy, well Freddy has only ever had eyes for one guy." She looked at me knowingly.

I studied her face, trying to understand what she was saying. Then it dawned on me. "You mean Vito?"

She nodded.

"I thought that was all in the past," I said.

"It was."

But the way she was looking at me made me wonder. I said, "Still?"

There was sadness in Minnie's eyes. She said, "Yes, angel. I'm afraid so."

19

———

When I got home from the Dome Room, I spent more time telling Vito parts of what Minnie had revealed to me than Minnie had spent telling me in the first place. It took longer, because Vito kept interrupting me. He made comments about Father Whalen, about Pearl Harbor, and about Leonard Lehnert. He told me what he thought about cops, and what he'd heard about the Dome Room.

I omitted telling Vito about meeting George, the accountant. More importantly, I chose not to reveal the one thing Minnie shared with me that would matter to Vito the most. I didn't mention that Freddy was still in love with him. I wasn't sure what Vito would do if he knew how Freddy still felt.

I did tell Vito, though, that my friend Maurice was a

regular at the Dome and that he called it the 'do me' room.

Vito snickered at that. "Maurice, eh? When am I going to meet this buddy of yours?" he asked.

We'd been in our living room when I began telling him about my visit to the Dome Room. By the time I got around to mentioning Maurice, we'd made our way up to the bedroom. Vito was now sitting on the edge of the bed in his t-shirt. He still had on his pants and shoes. I'd already put on my pajamas and climbed under the covers to watch my favorite show: Vito undressing. I was propped up on a pillow, the better to observe him. Vito's next step would be to take off his shoes. Then his pants. Vito never wore pajamas.

Before he met me, Vito always slept in the nude. But over time I'd convinced him that when we were together I'd go crazy if he didn't wear *something* in bed —underwear, if nothing else. At first he thought I was kidding. But eventually I convinced him that if he was lying next to me naked all night, I'd never be able to sleep. He asked why I didn't just close my eyes. I told him it was because I had other senses besides sight, and when my body brushed against his, even if it was just my hand, the rest of me was electrified because I knew he was naked.

"We could meet Maurice at the Dome Room sometime," I ventured. "Minnie's a lot of laughs. And she puts on a great show."

"Maybe," said Vito. "But I'm not an 'Over the Rainbow' kind of guy."

"You like musicals, don't you?"

"No. I like opera." Vito had just finished taking off his shoes. Now he stood up. "Why would I settle for a cheap imitation?"

"You're such a snob!"

Vito smiled as he turned to face me, unbuckled his belt and let his pants fall to the floor. He knew what I liked. "I am," he said. "I like high-class art and good-looking men."

"Oh, yeah?"

"Yeah!" He said with a sly leer.

I grabbed the pillow next to me and threw it at his chest. He caught it and pretended to be knocked backward. But then after staggering and wobbling around, he fell forward onto the bed.

For some reason, his mentioning good-looking 'men' in the plural made me think of Freddy. Straining for an air of innocence, I said, "I bet Freddy likes show tunes."

"Frederick!" Vito sneered. "What does he have to do with anything?" Vito crawled up on the bed beside me. "The man is a walking stereotype. He likes all that kind of stuff. But let's please not talk about him. OK?"

"Fine," I said. "If that's how you want it."

"I do."

I turned on my pillow to face him. "Then what about Father Whalen? I have to go see him. I have to do it for work. Minnie said he's at the Church of the Holy Family. But I don't know how to go about it. I've never actually been in a Catholic church. I guess the priests live in a rectory, right? But is that inside the church or in a separate building?"

"It's in a separate building," Vito said. "But usually nearby. You shouldn't have any trouble finding it."

"It would be nice if you came with me to see him," I said. "You could be my guide."

Vito shook his head. "I don't want to see that snake," he said. "Why do you think I left the funeral parlor so fast? He gives me the creeps."

"But what if I can't recognize him?" I really wasn't sure if I would. "All priests look the same to me."

"Oh, come on." Vito almost laughed. "Don't give me that. You saw him. And I'm sure you'd recognize him, seeing as he's not bad looking. You just want to drag me deeper into this."

"Well, yes, I do." I touched his arm. "But why not? If Father Whalen did all these things Minnie says he did, don't you think we should expose him?"

"We?"

"You're the one he pestered at Pearl Harbor. *You* have more of a personal stake in this than I do."

"What Whalen did to me was trivial."

"Maybe. But what he did to the others wasn't. What happened to Ray McDonald and to that other sailor Ray was caught with was not trivial."

Vito was quiet for a moment. Then he threw his

head back on his pillow. He had a distant look in his eyes. "I blame the Navy for that as much as I blame Whalen." He propped himself up, leaned his head against the headboard, then turned to face me. "The Navy was happy enough to have us fight and die—as long as we kept our heads down and pretended to be something phony. The brass were always going on about how we were defending 'freedom.' But that only meant freedom for some men. For some of us it wasn't the kind of freedom that meant we were free to be ourselves."

"Well then," I said. "If you let creeps like Whalen get away with forcing people to do things against their wishes, how are you any better?"

Vito rolled his eyes. "Talk about hitting below the belt."

'Well? Will you come with me or not?"

"Fine! I'll take you to the church."

He turned to say something more, but before he could, I bobbed up and kissed him firmly on the mouth. The kiss went on for a while. Eventually, while the kiss continued to go on, my hands got busy and Vito's underwear, almost of its own accord, came off.

20

It was 10:15 a.m. on Wednesday morning when we arrived at the Church of the Holy Family. Vito had telephoned the church office and found out that confessions were heard on Wednesdays, during what they called the Holy Hour of Eucharistic Adoration, from five to six p.m., or by appointment with one of the parish priests. Since Vito didn't want anyone else around during his visit, he'd made an appointment to see Father Whalen for confession at 10:30 Wednesday morning. He'd told the church office that his confession was urgent and that he couldn't come later in the day.

When he made the appointment, the secretary asked for a name to write down. Vito told her to write down 'Mr. Foster.' He knew that Freddy had never been to Pearl Harbor. And he was confident that Freddy had never been inside a church of any kind. If

Father Whalen happened to recognize Freddy's name on his appointment list as being the name of a cast member of *The Shadow's Voice*, so much the better. Vito figured Whalen would be all the more intrigued.

When we entered the church, we saw two women kneeling side by side at a pew midway down the sanctuary. There was no one else in the church. The women were praying. They didn't look up as we walked quietly into the back of the sanctuary.

The sanctuary itself was enormous. Light flooded in from large stained glass windows flanking the altar. The walls of the church were elaborately painted and stenciled. The vaulted ceilings were supported by sculpted columns and arches. The pews that filled the sanctuary, the communion railing at the front, and the confessionals at the side were all made of ornately-carved dark wood.

The confessionals themselves were intricately designed structures with three doors, one in the middle and one at each end. The center door bore a carving of Christ on the cross. The door was flanked on either side by marble statues on pedestals. This center door was meant for the priest to use. At both ends of the confessional were curved doors with darkened glass that opened into the compartments meant for penitents to use.

"I've seen this style before," Vito whispered. "Inside his compartment, the priest has a window on each side with a sliding cover. He opens the cover to one side to hear the confession of the person on that side. Then when he's done with that person, he closes the cover and turns to the person on the other side and slides open that cover. That's how they keep things moving when there's a line of people waiting."

"Vito, what are you going to say when you get in there?" I asked.

"I'm going to start with a confession," he said. "I have to gain Whalen's trust."

"You mean a real confession?"

"Of course."

"Do you actually have something to confess?"

"Everybody has something to confess, Elliot, even me. Why do you ask?"

"Because I was thinking maybe I could go into the booth at the other end and … you know … listen in. I really want to hear what Whalen has to say."

Vito wrinkled his forehead. "I don't know, Elliot."

"But if what you have to confess is private, I guess I should stay out of it."

Vito thought about it. Then he said, "What I'm planning to say to Whalen is personal to him and to me. I'm going to talk about what happened in the library at Pearl Harbor. But you already know about that."

"I do."

"So, I suppose …" He lowered his head and ran his hand through his hair. I could see he was struggling to make up his mind. He looked up again. "I suppose if you want to try to listen in, it's OK with me. But you have to be quiet. He can't know you're there."

"I understand. I'll be very quiet."

"And you'll have to wait until I've already gone into the booth. Otherwise, he might start with you."

"OK. I'll wait a few beats before I go."

"Do *you* have something to confess, Elliot?"

"I … uh … I suppose I do. It's like you said. Everybody does."

"Is there anything you want to tell me?"

"Oh, Vito … I … I think at some point … I want to tell you more about myself."

"Really?"

"Yes." I nodded.

"But not right now?"

'Not right this minute," I said. "And not here. I'm not used to being in a place like this. Everything feels so weighty here."

"It's a hallowed space," said Vito. "People come here to grapple with life's most important questions."

"I really appreciate you doing this," I said. "I know the church played a big role in your life."

"More than you know."

"And I know you're doing this for me, to help with the investigation."

"It's not just your claim investigation. I've been carrying a grudge against Whalen … and against the church, really. I want to let go of it. Maybe doing this will help me wipe the slate clean."

I looked down the aisle to the confessional. "Do you think he's already in there waiting for you?"

"There's only one way to find out. I'm going in."

Vito made his way down the aisle past the praying women. When he got to the confessional, he stopped at the first door. After pausing a moment, he continued walking past the middle door and on to the door at the far end of the confessional. There he stopped and looked back at me with an impish look on his face. He opened the door and went inside.

If I was going to try to hear Vito's confession, I knew I had to act quickly. I stood and walked down the aisle. As I passed the praying women, one of them turned to glance at me. When I got to the first door of the confessional I saw why Vito had not used it. There was a small sign affixed to the door handle that said 'Closed for Repair.' I hesitated. I looked back at the woman who'd glanced at me. She turned her head away and closed her eyes again.

I pulled softly on the door handle. As silently as possible, I opened the door, stepped inside and closed it. I crouched down and tried to get my bearings in the darkness of the chamber. After a moment I was able to make out the reason that the booth was closed. There was a split in the wood in the partition six inches below the sliding cover. It looked as if someone had kneed or kicked it, causing the panel to crack. As a result there was an irregular slit separating two panels in the wood.

I kneeled and scrunched down low enough to be able to peer through the slit. I saw Father Whalen's lap. No one was speaking. I heard a slight rapping sound, which sounded like Vito knocking on the partition from his side of the booth. Then Father Whalen shifted sideways a bit more and slid open the cover between his chamber and Vito's. I quickly put my ear to the slit so that I could hear what they said.

Vito said, "I confess to Almighty God and to you, Father, that I have sinned."

"When was your last confession?" Whalen asked.

"I can't remember."

"Can you remember approximately?"

"Yes." Vito paused. "It was during the war."

"So it's been a few years?"

"Yes."

"Why so long?"

"Something happened during the war, Father, that caused me to lose my faith."

"I see."

"That's the reason I'm here now. I want to talk about it."

"All right. Tell me what caused you to lose your faith, my son."

"I was stationed in Pearl Harbor. At the naval base."

At this point Vito paused. I turned my head back to look through the slit again. I saw Father Whalen lift himself slightly from his seat and move his head until it was just above the opening to Vito's chamber. He appeared to be gazing down from a higher and closer angle in order to get a better look through the grate at Vito's face. Then he sat back down. He said, "You say you were at Pearl Harbor at the naval base. Were you a sailor?"

"Yes. I was," Vito said. "And I was on the base awaiting deployment."

"I see."

"At the time I was, as you can imagine, quite young and naive. I had been raised a Catholic. I went to church every week."

"And you were sincere? In your faith?" Whalen asked.

"Yes," Vito said. "I was interested in astronomy, and whenever I got a chance I tried to learn more about it. My faith grew out of a natural wonder at the beauty and vastness of the universe."

"So what happened? Did you somehow lose your faith to science?"

"No, Father. I'm just telling you why I had faith. My interest in astronomy also explains why I happened to go to the library on base one day."

"The library?"

"Yes, Father. I went to the library to look for books about astronomy. I found one and brought the book to one of the tables in the library reading room to read it."

There was another pause. Neither man spoke. I turned to look through the slit, and I saw Father

Whalen try once more to get a clearer look at Vito. But he said nothing.

Then Vito continued. "As it happened, another man came to the table and sat down next to me."

"Someone you knew?"

"Only indirectly. The man was a chaplain. I had seen him before at one of the Sunday services on the base."

Again there was a pause where neither man spoke.

Finally, Whalen said, "So I gather you were still going to services at this time?"

"Yes, I was."

"Did you speak to the chaplain?"

"No. We didn't speak. But I thought it was odd that he sat next to me. There were empty chairs on both sides of the table. There was no one else sitting at the table. He could have easily sat across from me, but he sat next to me."

There was now a long and awkward silence. Through the slit I saw that Father Whalen had his hands clenched and that he'd begun to fidget in his seat. But he said nothing.

Finally, Vito broke the silence. He asked, "Why do you think he did that, Father?"

Father Whalen cleared his throat and said, "Well, perhaps the chaplain was being friendly. I believe that's part of their mission, to make friends with servicemen, to get to know them." Then he paused and said, "What do you think?"

"I think you're right. I think he was being friendly."

Now Father Whalen's voice showed some irritation. He asked, "Why are you telling me this?"

"Because it was what happened next that caused me to lose my faith."

Once again a long, awkward silence ensued. I stared at Father Whalen's hands clenching and unclenching.

"What happened?" he finally asked. "What could possibly have happened, my son?" He spoke with a mix of irritation and anxiety in his voice.

"I was reading my astronomy book. I had both of my hands on the book on the table in front of me. The man next to me, the chaplain, also had a book lying on the table in front of him. But he only had one of his hands on the book: his left hand. His right hand was hanging down by his side. He was sitting to my left."

"What's your point?"

"I didn't think much of it at first. But then I noticed his knuckles were brushing very slightly against the side of my left leg."

"So you're saying you happened to be sitting close together, side by side?"

"Yes. But then his hand stopped bumping on my leg. He just held his hand where it was, which was barely touching my leg."

"I don't understand. Why are you telling me these details?"

"So you can get a picture of what happened. So you can feel what it was like from my point of view."

"What did you feel?"

"Gradually, almost imperceptibly, the pressure of his hand touching my leg grew stronger."

Now Father Whalen raised his voice slightly. "Well? What did you do? Did you move away?"

"No, Father. I didn't."

"And why not?"

"Because I … I found myself getting aroused."

Father Whalen stopped clenching his hands together and now clenched his right thigh with his right hand. His voice rose higher and almost cracked. "Aroused?"

"Yes, Father. I could tell that the man was touching my leg on purpose and it awakened a feeling inside me."

Whalen lifted himself up off his chair, peering now down through the grate from a higher angle still, as if he was trying to peep at the bottom half of Vito's body. "A sexual feeling?"

"Yes."

There was a long pause. I saw Whalen sit back down. He let his head fall down to his hands. He was silent for several moments. Then he lifted his head up and spoke through the grate. He asked, "Do you remember what the chaplain looked like?"

"Yes, Father. I remember him very clearly."

"And you … you're telling me … you're saying you were attracted to him?"

"Well. I hadn't thought I was. But then when he

touched my leg, I realized I couldn't control my thoughts."

"What thoughts?"

"I was far from home. I hadn't had sex in a very long time. But I still had desires. And then right at that point I felt his hand begin to slide up my leg."

"On top of your leg?"

"Yes, Father. He slid his hand very slowly up onto the top of my leg, about midway between my knee and my groin."

"Why would he do that?"

"I think he wanted to seduce me, Father. He began to move his hand along the top of my leg, sliding it very gradually, very gently. He moved it from my knee toward my groin. Each little bit he moved caused me to feel a growing desire."

"So you were aroused by this?"

"Yes, I was. I was very aroused. And I was young so my arousal was intense enough so that it was evident in the fabric of my pants, Father."

"He saw this?"

"He couldn't see it. Neither one of us spoke. Neither one of us moved our heads. So he couldn't possibly have seen my physical reaction, which was hidden beneath the table."

"So the chaplain didn't know you had that reaction?"

"No. He didn't. And then something happened so that he never found out."

"What happened?"

"Another sailor came by and just by chance he sat down at the table across from us."

"Ah."

"So then I stood up. But as I stood up I turned away very quickly, so neither the chaplain nor the other sailor could see my erection."

"You turned away?"

"Yes. I did. And I grunted something. I was very brusque in my tone. I think the chaplain never knew how close he came to succeeding."

I saw that Father Whalen was sliding his right hand along the top of his leg, almost in imitation of what he'd heard described by Vito.

Father Whalen leaned into the grate and asked, "Did you see this chaplain again?"

"No, Father. Not after that. Not for many years," Vito said.

"So this was the situation that caused you to lose your faith?"

"Yes, Father. I never went to church again."

"Why not?"

"Because I realized then that … that it was all an illusion."

"An illusion?"

"Yes. The moral teaching. The admonition against sin. It was a lie."

Father Whalen said, "Everyone sins, my son."

"Over the years," Vito said, "that has become very clear to me."

"Could you not repent?"

"I repented my faith, Father. But I did not repent my arousal."

"What do you mean?"

"I mean I went on to have many more moments of arousal. With many more men."

"What are you saying? Are you saying that you still have these immoral feelings?"

"Yes."

"And are you still acting upon these feelings?"

"Yes, I am. I do so all the time."

"And you do not repent?"

"No."

"Then I cannot absolve you."

"Do you ever repent *your* sins, Father?"

"Of course I do. Why would you ask that?"

"Because some people think all they have to do is repent and then they can go right on with the sin, as if they can start over with a clean slate. But that's not right. That's not sincere contrition, not if you're going to keep on doing the same thing."

"You're right, my son. You must repent sincerely. But the flesh is weak."

"I know the flesh is weak. That's why I still sometimes think about the chaplain, Father."

"After all this time?" Whalen paused, then in a quiet voice he asked, "In what way?"

"He wore a different kind of uniform, an officer's uniform. I have since then found myself responding to … well … authority."

"Erotically?"

"Yes."

"To the authority of an officer?"

"Yes … or … or to the authority of a priest …," said Vito.

"What are you saying?"

"The truth is, Father, I fantasize about confessing something to a priest. I imagine telling him about my attractions, just as I'm telling you now. But then in my fantasy he responds."

"The priest? Responds how?"

"He leaves his chamber. He comes into mine."

"Oh? Just like that, eh? And then what?"

"Then I stand up. And he kneels down."

"Why does he kneel?"

"Because I have a big cock, Father."

"Oh? And uh, uh, this is something you still fantasize about?"

"Yes, Father."

"Even now."

"Yes. Especially now."

"Why now?"

"Because my cock is hard right now, Father. And as I said, it's very big."

I saw Whalen stand up from his seat and lean down to whisper into the grate. "Do you want me to come into your chamber, my son, to offer you absolution?"

"I do."

I turned again to watch through the slit as Father Whalen opened his door. Then I heard the sound of another door opening. I could no longer see what was happening. But I knew that Father Whalen had just entered Vito's chamber.

I could hardly believe what was happening. Vito knew I was on the other side of the confessional listening in. I didn't see how any of this fit with Vito's plan. How was seducing Father Whalen going to lead to gaining new information about Leonard Lehnert? I stood up, opened the door of my chamber and stepped out.

21

——————

As soon as I stepped out of the confessional, I heard a loud bang as the door at the other end of the confessional whipped open. Vito burst out, dragging Father Whalen out with him. Vito looked as wild as he sometimes did in the ring. He spun Father Whalen around, then wound up his left arm and punched him hard in the jaw. Father Whalen shrieked and fell back onto the side of the pew.

Meanwhile, the women who'd been praying leapt to their feet when they heard the commotion. One of them immediately moved to the aisle and began to walk to the back of the church. The other one went to the aisle and stood looking at Father Whalen bent over the pew. She took a tentative step toward him. The other woman shouted at her, "Jenny," she said. "Come with me this instant!"

Jenny turned and walked toward the back of the church.

Now Vito pulled Father Whalen up off the pew and drew his arm back ready to punch him again.

"No! Wait! What do you want?"

Vito waited until the women left the church before he spoke. Then he said, "I want you to tell me the truth. What did you do to Leonard Lehnert?"

"To who?"

"To the man who was friends with your victim, Ray MacDonald."

"What are you talking about?"

"Don't lie to me! I know you know all about it. I saw you at Lehnert's funeral."

Father Whalen looked toward me, seeing me for the first time. He gave me a plaintive look, as if I would help him. Then he turned back to Vito. "Yes. I was at the funeral. I … I was just there because I …"

Vito smirked. "Because you were a fan of the radio show?"

"Yes. But not just because of that. I went because my friend, Father O'Connor, gave the eulogy. I went to the funeral with him."

"And what about Ray MacDonald?"

"What about him?"

"Where was he? Where is he?"

"I don't know anything about him."

"You knew enough to put the screws on him. You've

known all about him since Pearl Harbor. You got Ray to do things against his will."

"No. Nothing was against his will."

"Really?"

"He … well …" Father Whalen suddenly went quiet. He looked at me, then back at Vito. He seemed to be trying to put two and two together about us. Finally he said, "I guess you must know. Ray met Leonard. He stopped wanting to see me."

"And so you figured you'd put the touch on Leonard instead."

"What?"

"I heard all about it."

"From who?"

"From Minnie at the Dome Room. She told my friend there and he told me."

"You fellas don't understand. I just … I just."

"Oh, I understand," Vito said. "You just wanted someone to keep you happy. Just like you wanted me to make you happy in the library."

"I didn't do anything with anybody who didn't want the same thing. You said so yourself. You just told me I was right. I was right to sit next to you. You were aroused."

Vito grimaced and glanced at me. "No, Father. I lied about that just now. I was repulsed by you."

Father Whalen's head fell back. As if Vito's insult hit him as hard as Vito's fist had.

Vito continued, "If I had wanted you, I'd have gone

with you. And you would have put the screws on me to keep coming back to you the same way you put them on Ray MacDonald."

"Is that what you think? Is that why you hit me?"

"Yes. Because you are the lowest of the low. You are a rank hypocrite."

"I told you. Everyone sins. Even priests. You don't know what my life is like."

"Where is Ray?"

"I don't know. I swear."

"What did you do to Leonard?"

"To Leonard? Nothing. Absolutely nothing. How could I have done anything to him? He died in an accident. His wife says so. She was right there on the boat with him. What are you implying?"

"I'm implying that if Leonard killed himself it was because of you. Because you threatened to destroy his career, to humiliate him in front of the world."

"No, I ... I'm sure it was an accident. He didn't kill himself."

"Are you sure? Is that why you came to the funeral?"

"I just wanted to talk to his wife. To hear what happened directly from her."

"And did you?"

"Yes. She confirmed everything. She said it was an accident. Everyone says so, even the insurance company. She told me."

At this point the conversation was interrupted by sounds coming from the front of the church. The two women had come back and they'd brought another priest with them. He came rushing down the aisle toward me and Vito and Father Whalen.

Father Whalen called the name of the other priest, "Father O'Connor!"

Father O'Connor slowed his pace as he approached us. "What's going on?"

Father Whalen looked down, embarrassed. "I had an accident. I fell."

"Your mouth is bleeding."

"I tripped coming out of the confessional. I fell onto the pew. This gentleman was helping me."

Father O'Connor looked at Vito and then at me.

"Which gentleman?"

Father Whalen looked up and pointed at Vito. "This one."

Father O'Connor turned to me. "And who are you?"

"I'm a friend," I said. "My friend came to say his confession. I was waiting for him to finish."

"Did you see what happened?"

"Yes," I said. "It was just as the Father said. He fell onto a pew after coming out of the confessional. I guess he tripped. My friend tried to grab him … to catch him."

Father O'Connor turned to the two women. "Is that what you saw? I thought you said they were fighting."

"I don't know," said the one named Jenny. "It happened so fast. I was praying."

"What do you say?" Father O'Connor asked the other woman.

"I, too, was praying," she said. "I had my eyes closed. I heard what sounded like a scuffle. I saw only what took place after I opened them, which was Father Whalen falling onto the pew. It made quite a racket." She looked at Father Whalen. "Undoubtedly whatever Father Whalen says is correct." Her tone was arch.

After Vito and I left the church, I said, "When I saw Father Whalen for the first time at the funeral the other night I was surprised by how he looked. From what you'd told me about him in the past I was expecting someone old and unattractive. But he's not. Maybe he's not as good-looking as you are, but he's still good-looking if you ask me. Why did you call him repulsive?"

"When did I say that?"

"Just now. You told him you'd lied to him. You said you weren't aroused by him but repulsed by him when he made a pass at you at the library."

"Did I? I don't remember."

"You said something like that."

"Well, if I did, I wasn't talking about the way he looks. I was talking about his character."

"But you didn't know about his character back then, did you?"

"No. But I was already upset with another priest. Whalen making a pass at me was like a slap in the face after what the other priest did. What I never told you was that when I first got to Pearl Harbor I was still a practicing Catholic. There was another Catholic priest on the base whose name was Father Carroll. He was the last priest I confessed to before today."

"And that's who upset you?"

"I confessed to Father Carroll that I'd performed a sexual act with another sailor, but that I had repented and wanted absolution."

"You repented? Really?"

"Yes, really! I remember the words I spoke. 'Oh, my God, I am heartily sorry for having offended Thee.' I was truly remorseful. I'd offended God, God himself! I was still a sap who believed in the Church back then."

"So what happened?"

"Father Carroll spat on me through the grate in the confessional."

"Whoa! Are they allowed to do that?"

"No. They're not. They're supposed to forgive everyone who confesses and repents: adulterers, thieves, murderers, you name it. That's the whole point of confession and repentance. But not only did this guy spit on me, he wouldn't absolve me; he told me I made him sick. Then he stormed out of the confessional before I could say anything. That's when I quit the church for good. That's what forced me to face up to what I really believed. And what I really believed deep inside was that God could not be offended by my nature. I didn't choose to be the way I am. God made me who I am. How could it be otherwise? And how could who I am offend Him? After that, I no longer wanted to be part of a church that wanted me to repent for who God made me." Vito paused for a moment, then added, "Maybe I ought to have thanked Father Carroll. He was the one who opened my eyes. He let me see that the church's idea of sin was a sham."

"My parents never took me to church."

"You're lucky."

"But how does this relate to Father Whalen?"

"It was two days after Father Carroll spat on me that Father Whalen tried to seduce me in the library. When I realized what Whalen was doing, I was steamed. Those priests are total hypocrites. That's why he repulsed me."

I nodded. "I understand." Then I thought about the reason we'd come to the church in the first place. "When Father O'Connor came to see what was going on just now, you went along with Whalen when he said he'd tripped. I thought we came here to expose him."

"I changed my mind."

"What? How come?"

"I felt sorry for the guy."

"You felt sorry for him? You just punched him."

"Yeah, I did. But I didn't like how it made me feel."

"Why's that?"

"Because I started thinking, Whalen's just another guy like us."

"But look what he did. He forced guys to have sex with him! That's not like us."

"I know. I know." Vito nodded. "That's why I hit him. But he … he's really trapped, when you think about it."

"Why? Because he's a priest?"

"Yeah, and because all of us are trapped. None of us has any rules to follow. I think he's been going at it from the only angle he figures he can use."

"Well, he's still a creep if you ask me."

"I know, but what's the point of ruining his life?"

"He ruined Ray MacDonald's life. And Leonard Lehnert's, too, for all we know."

"Yeah, I suppose he did." Vito stopped and turned to face me. "But look," he said, "As you know, I used to be a fall guy for Winkler. I was forced to do things I didn't want to do, the same as those guys. What Whalen did to Ray MacDonald is no different than what Winkler did to me. But after Winkler died I finally caught on to how he really felt. I think he loved me in his own way. He left me his house for Christ's sake. And it makes me think, you can't know what's going on inside these guys."

I shrugged. "Maybe."

"Anyway, I'm not an eye for an eye kind of fellow," Vito added.

As we continued walking, I thought about what I ought to do next. "So where does that leave us?" I asked.

"What are you talking about?"

"I'm talking about Gloria Lehnert's death claim."

Vito looked puzzled. "You think Whalen was involved?"

"Not according to him. He just said he had nothing to do with Leonard Lehnert's death. He said he's certain Leonard didn't commit suicide. And he swore he has no idea where Ray MacDonald is."

"I believe him," Vito said. "What's his motive? Why would he want to get rid of Lehnert or lose track of MacDonald? There's nothing in it for him either way."

"So what should I do? Drop the investigation? Pay the claim?"

"I think you should keep looking for Ray MacDonald. His not coming to the funeral doesn't add up. Maybe there's a good reason. But it makes me wonder what he's up to."

"How am I supposed to find him?"

Vito rubbed his chin. "Maybe you should talk to your friend Minnie. She's the one who seems to know the most about him."

Vito was right. Minnie had told me that as far as she knew Ray was still in Chicago. It was certainly possible that she'd seen or heard from Ray since we last spoke. Or maybe she'd heard something from another patron at the Dome Room. I decided I'd pay her a visit during her next appearance.

22

———

I met Minnie at the Dome Room on Friday night, an hour before her set began. Everything at the Dome Room was the same as it had been three days before. Walt, the bartender, was pouring drinks in his black coat and tie. George, the accountant, sat on stool number six giving the once-over to every man who came in. I said hello to George, and then Minnie and I took seats at the same table we'd sat at three days earlier.

I began by telling Minnie about Vito's encounter with Father Whalen.

Minnie ate the story up. "Vito actually punched him?"

I nodded. "He did. And you know he's a boxer. He let go with a left uppercut punch." I made my left hand into a fist and thrust it up hard toward my jaw by way of demonstration. "Whalen flew back into the pews."

She smiled. "I hate to say it, but I like picturing that. The louse got what was coming to him."

"After he hit him, Vito said he felt sorry for the guy."

"Oh, yeah? Why's that?"

"He said Whalen is just trapped ... like the rest of us ... in a situation with no good angles."

She mulled that over. "I think maybe I'd like to spend some time with Vito one of these days. I go for tough guys who are softies. And seeing how you and Freddy feel about him, I feel I ought to get to know him. Why don't you bring him around sometime?"

"I'll bring him around. But only if you promise you won't actually go for him."

Minnie laughed. "Why not, angel? Are you afraid I might get somewhere?"

"With Vito? No. Impossible!"

"Then what does it matter? I go for all you guys."

"Is that so?" I tilted my head. "Have you ever landed one of us?"

Minnie put a mischievous look in her eyes. "That's for me to know and you to find out."

"Oh, it's like that, is it?"

"Yeah."

"I think I ought to read your diary. Everyone says you like to zig and zag."

"Oh, I do, angel. And I have very simple rules. I like boys who like boys and girls who like girls. The trouble is, the boys who like boys are tricky to rope in when you're not a boy."

"What about boys who like girls? I bet you wouldn't have a hard time roping in one of them."

"Yeah, well … I'm afraid the boys who like girls have too much animal and not enough magnetism for my taste."

We sat in silence for a minute and sipped our drinks. Before coming to the Dome, I'd decided to ask Minnie about the ending of "The Fortune-Teller." I'd listened to every episode of *The Shadow's Voice* for years. It bothered me to have missed the ending to that one. I thought if I was going to find out how the episode ended, I'd better ask about it while she could still remember what happened. I was also curious to know how the handoffs between Roger and Freddy had worked out during the live broadcast.

"Do you remember when I came to the studio and watched you rehearse?" I asked.

She nodded. "Sure. It was the rehearsal for last week's episode."

"I left before you finished. And then I missed the live broadcast, because I had to go to the morgue. So I never heard how the story ended. Do you remember the episode?"

"I remember the night you visited," she said. "But at the moment I don't remember which script we did that night. We do a new one every week."

"It was the first show you did after Leonard died. Carl said the episode was called 'The Fortune-Teller.'"

"Oh, right. And that was Freddy and Roger's first attempt at trading off the roles, wasn't it?"

"It was. I know it was because I had just suggested the idea to Carl."

"The trade-off was your idea?"

"It was. Didn't you know?"

"No. I didn't." Minnie shook her head. "Now Freddy will have another reason to hate you. That was supposed to be his role. He was the understudy."

"Carl told me he didn't think Freddy could do the tough guy voice."

"Oh, angel, he could've done it. But Carl never gave him a chance. Carl hears the way Freddy sounds in real life and he can't get past it. You know what? Carl's a stick in the mud. He thinks we're all too theatrical. He thinks all of us except Roger put too much zing in our voices. I tell him 'That's what people want. They want pizzazz. I mean, for Christ's sake, the audience is sitting at home with the damn lights turned out. We don't want them to fall asleep!' But, oh no. We're all too peppy for Carl's taste."

I couldn't disagree with her. "I, for one, love how you sound," I said. "You always make me believe you, whether you're playing an old lady or a babe in the woods."

"Thank you, angel! Though I'm not sure I have a babe-in-the-woods voice. Unless you mean I sound like a 'babe' even when my character is in the woods." She took a sip of her drink. Then she said, "Anyway, getting back to "The Fortune-Teller." Was that the episode where a guy named Grayson hires Percy to find his wife, Rose?"

"Yes. That was it."

"How much of it did you hear?"

I began to recount what I remembered of the episode. "When Percy gets to Grayson's house, Grayson tells him that Rose has been seeing a fortune-teller."

"A fortune-teller named Madam Delilah, which was my role."

"Right, and then Percy tracks down Madam Delilah for an interview in his gossip columnist disguise. That's as far as I got."

"OK."

"So what happened next?"

Minnie tilted her head back as she recalled the story. "Let's see," she said. "After his interview with Madam Delilah, Percy goes back to see Grayson. But when he gets to Grayson's house, he finds Grayson lying dead on the floor." She paused. "And then … something happens." She scrunched up her forehead and took another sip of her drink. "Let's see … there was a sound effect that Bob had to keep redoing. Oh, right. Percy hears the sound of high heels walking down the stairs in Grayson's house. Clop. Clop. Clop." Minnie imitated the sound effect from the show. "It turns out the heels belong to Rose. Remember her? She was Grayson's missing wife."

I remembered. "She was also the woman he saw on the streetcar?"

Minnie nodded. "Yes. So now she comes down the stairs and points a gun at Percy. She admits she's killed her husband. She says she had to kill him. She says he was an evil man. She says now the only thing left is to take her own life. But before Percy can do anything, she uses the gun to force him into a chair while she ties him up. Then Percy hears her take off in her car. Percy struggles with his bonds and tips the chair over. There's a lot of sound effects. It's all very tense. Finally, Percy manages to cut himself loose with a pocket knife. But it's too late. She's gone. Later the cops find her car with a dead body inside. It crashed into the Chicago River."

"Rose dies?"

"So it seems. But that's where Percy gets clever. He has a hunch that the body in the car is really Madam Delilah. And he's right! It turns out, Rose paid Madam Delilah to leave town, then she killed her and staged her own suicide using Madam Delilah's body to throw off the police."

"So Rose is still alive?"

"Yes. And Percy tracks her down at her new apartment on the South Side. And then, of course, he waits in the dark for her to come home."

"Which is when she hears the shadow's voice."

Minnie smiled. "And then, like all the killers before her, she knows the game is up."

As I thought about the story, it reminded me of what happened to Leonard. It seemed significant that the story was written just before he died. I asked, "Did Leonard and Gloria both work on that script?"

Minnie nodded. "Yes. They wrote it together."

"And it's about a murderer who stages a phony suicide by using someone else's body?"

"Yeah, so what?"

"Doesn't that seem coincidental?"

"What are you talking about?"

"I'm talking about Leonard's death."

Minnie looked confused. "Leonard's death was an accident, not a suicide."

"But what if it wasn't? What if Gloria rigged it so that it just looked like an accident?"

"How could she? Carl saw the whole thing!"

"Yes, but she could have knocked Leonard overboard on purpose."

"Oh, angel, that's ridiculous." Minnie made a face. "You think she killed him?"

"Maybe."

"It would be a nutty way to do it. Leonard knew how to swim. She'd be nuts to knock him overboard and expect him to drown."

I'd actually considered this before. Minnie was right. It would be a crazy way to try to kill someone. "I agree." I said. "So I have another theory. What if Leonard didn't drown? What if it was all a hoax to make everyone think he died?"

"What would be the point of that?"

"To get the insurance money."

Minnie shook her head. "That doesn't make any sense. They didn't need the insurance money. They were sitting pretty just on what he was making from the show. Why would they give that up?"

I rubbed the back of my neck. "There's something else. And maybe it's more important than the insurance money. There's another big coincidence in this case. Leonard died just when Father Whalen was about to extort him. Maybe Leonard's death was staged for Father Whalen's benefit."

Minnie stared at me. "You mean so he'd stop extorting Leonard and Ray?"

"Right."

Minnie took this in. "And then what? Leonard and Ray ran away together to start a new life somewhere else?"

"Why not? That's what Rose Grayson tries to do in the script."

Minnie slowly nodded. "So, OK. Maybe what you're saying is possible. But then what happened to Leonard? If he's not dead, what happened after he fell off the boat?"

"He could have just swum out of sight."

"But nobody saw him after he fell. He'd have had to have swum underwater the whole way."

"He didn't have to swim underwater all the way back to shore. It was getting dark. He could have come up for air after he'd gotten far enough away from the other boats so no one could see him."

"And then what? He'd still have to swim all the way back to shore after that. And like I said, angel, it's a long way. I don't think he was that good of a swimmer."

I thought about that. I remembered my trip out to the lake on a Wendella boat when I was investigating the Winkler case. "You know what? There's a breakwater out there. That means Leonard only had to swim as far as the breakwater. Then he could have hidden behind it. It's made of huge rocks. It wouldn't be hard to hide behind one of them."

Minnie shrugged. "I guess that's possible."

"In fact, at that point, he wouldn't have to swim any further. He could have almost walked back to the shore by making his way on top of the breakwater."

"Maybe. But you're forgetting one thing," Minnie said. "Leonard's body turned up in the Chicago River. The police found it. You saw it."

"I saw *someone's* body."

"Yeah. OK." Minnie leaned forward. "But if that wasn't Leonard, then who was it?"

I raised my eyebrows. "Well, maybe they did something like in 'The Fortune-Teller' episode."

"What are you saying? That they killed someone, the way Rose killed Madam Delilah in their script?"

"Think about it," I said. "How else would they get a body that looked like Leonard's? Just like in the script, they'd have had to have found someone who looked like Leonard and then bumped him off."

Minnie looked horrified. She shook her head. "No!" She rapped her hand on the table. "I can't believe they'd do that."

"How else?"

Minnie tilted her head from side to side as she thought about it. "I don't know. Maybe they just happened to find a body somewhere."

I frowned. "Nobody just happens to find a body. And even if they did, it wouldn't just happen to look like Leonard. That's absurd."

"I know. But it's the only thing that makes sense. Gloria and Leonard are not murderers." She was silent for a moment as she thought more about it. "Besides, who knows if the body actually looked like Leonard. Gloria was the one who identified it. She could have just lied."

"I was there. I saw it."

"What you just said was you saw *someone's* body. Did anyone who knew him see the body? I mean, besides Gloria."

I nodded. "Vito saw it."

"When?"

"At the funeral."

"How? The casket was closed."

"Vito lifted the lid when no one was looking. It was before you got there."

"Are you kidding?"

"No, I'm not kidding. He said the body looked like Leonard's, but he wasn't completely sure because he hadn't seen Leonard since high school." I hesitated. "Vito checked something else and based on that he thinks it was definitely not Leonard."

"Checked for what? A birthmark?"

"Yeah, uh … something like that. Vito and Leonard were on the wrestling team together. So Vito knew his particulars."

Minnie sipped her drink as she thought about this. "OK," she said. "But that just adds more weight to the idea that the whole thing was staged."

I was astonished to hear Minnie come to this conclusion. We were spinning theories based on hints from a radio script. But there was no denying that something was not as it seemed. The body part Vito had assessed was proof of that. But what kind of proof was it? I thought about whether or not there was any way I could prove that Leonard had feigned his own death. If it was a sham, the sham had to have been staged by Leonard and Gloria. The only way I could think of proving it was by tricking Gloria into confessing. I said, "Maybe if I went to Gloria and told her I knew Leonard's accident was a hoax and that she and Leonard had staged it, she'd break down and confess."

Minnie shook her head. "Maybe. But Gloria is pretty stubborn. I don't think she'd have tried a stunt like this if she wasn't sure she could pull it off."

"Then what can I do? There's no way to prove what happened."

Minnie seemed lost in thought. After a moment she said, "You know, earlier tonight at the studio we rehearsed this week's episode, which uses another script that Gloria wrote. If what you're saying is true, if she put something from real life in her 'Fortune-Teller' script, then I think she might have used real-life elements in this week's episode, too."

"What elements?"

"That's what I'm sitting here trying to remember. I play an old lady named Mrs. Berk whose son is missing. The old lady hires Percy Ballard to find her son."

"And? Does he find the son?"

"He does. But there are little details in the episode about the son and his friend that make me wonder if she used details about Leonard and Ray that could be clues to what's going on."

"Like what?"

"The problem is I can't remember everything in the script. Gloria didn't include the gossip columnist version of Percy's character in this story. So Carl announced that Freddy wouldn't be reading any of Percy's lines. As you can imagine, Freddy had a fit. Throughout the rehearsal he was upset and kept interrupting Roger's lines. Freddy's my friend, so I tried to calm him down. But he was convinced that

Carl's decision was the first step toward giving the lead role permanently to Roger."

"Is Roger able to do the gossip columnist voice? I thought that was the whole reason Carl was using Freddy."

"Roger can do the dandy voice passably. He's not as good as Freddy. In fact, he sounds like the dullest dandy you ever heard. But I think it's good enough for Carl. I hate to say it, but Freddy's probably right. I'm afraid Carl's gonna pull Freddy out of the role altogether. The only reason Freddy was included in Ballard's role in the first place is because he was Leonard's understudy. But if Roger does all of Ballard's voices, Carl knows that would be less confusing for the audience."

"That's tough for Freddy."

"Yeah. But the point is, I was so distracted by Freddy's fits during the rehearsal, I don't remember all the details of the script. So when we perform the episode live tomorrow night, I'm gonna pay more attention."

"I can't wait to hear the show," I said.

23

At seven o'clock on Saturday night I usually turn off all the lights in the living room, then make myself comfortable in a chair next to the radio to listen to *The Shadow's Voice*. But this Saturday I kept the lights on. I wanted to be able to see well enough to jot down notes about the episode. I began my note-taking as soon as Alfred finished playing the show's opening theme music on the organ.

The episode began with the sound of a phone ringing. Minnie, who was playing the role of Mrs. Berk, started the dialogue. "Hello. This is Berk's gift shop," she said. "How may I help you?" Minnie paused, then said, "Oh yes, Mr. Porter, the paperweight? That was the one with the blue butterfly inside, wasn't it? Well, I'll have to … " Minnie stopped when a bell tinkled as someone opened the door of the gift shop. Then Minnie said, "Hold the line a moment, Mr.

Porter, I'll be right back." Next came the sound of footsteps. Minnie, sounding surprised, said, "Oh, Mr. Ballard, it's you. Do you have good news for me? Did you find my son?"

"I'm sorry, Mrs. Berk," Roger said in a serious tone. "Johnny is dead."

"Oh. Oh my. That can't be!"

"Take it easy, Mrs. Berk. Maybe you should take a seat."

Minnie, with emotion in her voice, said, "No. I … I … oh dear … will you give me a minute, Mr. Ballard. I was talking to a customer on the telephone just now. Let me finish that. Then I want to hear what you found out about my son."

Roger spoke the next lines in his narrator voice. "As Mabel Berk went back to the telephone, I thought about what I had to tell her. I thought about how it had all begun yesterday in my office, when that same gray-haired lady made her way to my desk, handed me an envelope, and asked me to find her son."

Minnie, reenacting the dialogue from the day before, picked it up from there. "His name is Johnny, Mr. Ballard. Well, nowadays he goes by John, now that he's grown up. He's twenty-four. One day, about a year ago, he left. He just disappeared. I haven't heard anything from him since. Not until that letter came yesterday addressed to him and postmarked from Madison, Wisconsin."

"Would you like to have a seat, Mrs. Berk?"

"Oh, thank you. Maybe I shouldn't have read Johnny's mail, Mr. Ballard. But it was the first clue I've had in a year that he was still alive. Will you read it?"

"All right," Roger said. Then he read the letter. "Dear John, It's taken longer than I thought, but the wait for our payout is finally over. Judy mailed me the papers. I got them this morning. So hurry up and get back to town and meet me at our favorite bar on Main Street at ten p.m. on Saturday night. Signed, Vance." Roger paused. "A bar on Main Street? What does that mean, Mrs. Berk."

"I don't know. I haven't a clue. I've never been to Madison," Minnie said. "But I don't like the idea of Johnny hanging out with Vance. To tell you the truth, it scares me."

"Does it? This fellow Vance said to meet him at ten p.m. Saturday night. That must be tonight!"

"It could be."

"Who is this Vance? Do you know him?"

"Oh, yes. I know him. He's Johnny's friend, Vance Stewart. Vance is one of those handsome boys that all the girls seem to like. You know the type: big muscles and a sweet face. Unfortunately, my Johnny fell in with him a few years ago. They became friends … sidekicks is what Johnny calls it. Now, it seems, they're always together."

"I see."

"I've never tried to choose Johnny's friends for him. Only I've always hoped he'd make friends with a nice, serious boy. You see, Johnny lost his father when he was six years old."

"My condolences, Mrs. Berk."

"It feels like a long time ago now," Minnie said wistfully. "It's been more than fifteen years."

"Getting back to this Vance Stewart," Roger said gently. "I take it he isn't the kind of friend you'd hoped Johnny would make?"

"No, Mr. Ballard. He's not. Vance is wild, much too wild. He's the kind of boy who rides a motorcycle; the kind who thinks a leather jacket makes him a tough guy. He's the sort of boy, Mr. Ballard, who thinks smoking smelly cigars is all it takes to be a grown man. You see, he doesn't have a father he can look up to either. Vance Stewart lost his father as a young boy just like Johnny did. I believe that's why he and Johnny were first drawn together."

"Where is Vance? Do you know?"

"No. I talked to Vance's mother after Johnny left. She told me Vance had left town, too. I just assumed the two boys ran off together."

"But if they ran off together, why would Vance mail Johnny a letter to your home here in Chicago?"

"That's what bothers me," Minnie said. "It doesn't make any sense. Whatever they're up to, I'm afraid Johnny and Vance have gotten into some kind of mischief with these papers he's talking about."

"You mean because the letter mentions a payout?"

"Yes. And because I know Vance Stewart. He's got

the idea that everyone but him is a sucker. He's what you'd call a con artist."

"If Vance Stewart thinks Johnny's back at home with you, maybe Johnny is somewhere nearby."

"That's what I'm hoping for. But where?"

"Do you know anything about these papers he mentions?"

"No, I don't, Mr. Ballard. That's why I want to hire you. Find out about these papers. And find my son."

"And that was how it all began," Roger said, returning to his narrator's voice. "That afternoon I got in my car and made the three-hour drive to Madison, Wisconsin. According to the attendant at a local gas station, there was only one bar on Main Street that any college age kid would bother going to. The bar was called 'Blackie's' and it had a reputation as being the kind of offbeat bar that college kids thought was hip. One of the main attractions at Blackie's was the jukebox. The owners had installed the latest Wurlitzer jukebox, called the Bubbler. The Bubbler was stocked with a variety of 78's. Most were the usual popular hits. But this particular jukebox also had a selection of opera records. It was just the kind of oddball thing that made a college kid feel like a grown-up."

Next came the sounds of a busy bar: clinking glasses, the chatter of people talking in the background, and the sound of an opera recording playing on the jukebox. In this case the aria was *Nessun*

Dorma from Puccini's opera *Turandot*. I recognized the tune because it's one of Vito's favorites.

At that point, Roger continued in his narrator voice. "I sat down at the bar at exactly 9:45 p.m. and ordered a double scotch. It didn't take me long to realize that I was sitting about 36 smelly inches away from a foul cigar. The cigar belonged to a good-looking kid in a leather jacket. I took a chance that the kid was Vance Stewart himself."

Now Roger switched back to his voice in character. "What kind of cigar is that, son? It smells like a stogie."

For the first time we heard the voice of the kid, played by Freddy. "What's it to you, Mister?"

"Oh, it's nothing really," Roger continued. "It's just that I couldn't help smelling it. Your cigar's got a strong smell."

"So what?"

"So nothing." Roger switched back into his narrator voice. "At that point I pulled out the fancy Havana cigar I'd bought at the cigar shop on the edge of town. I figured I might get a chance to make a play like this, so I'd prepared in advance." Roger changes back to his character voice. "Here, kid," he says. "Why don't you try smoking a real cigar for a change?"

"What's the gag?"

"No gag. It's what I do for a living. I'm in the market for a punk like you who's an eager-beaver."

"Oh, yeah?"

"Yeah. And if the punk takes my cigar, then I know he's got potential."

"Potential for what?"

"Potential to make some of that dough you said was missing in your life."

"Doing what?"

"I happen to have an operation coming up and I need some help with it."

"What kind of help?"

"I need a hot shot to do me a little favor that involves dropping off a package. Actually, I need two hot shots. You wouldn't happen to have a buddy you could work with, would you?"

'Suppose I do?"

"If you do, you could make an easy fifty bucks."

"Fifty each?"

"No, tiger, I mean twenty-five each. It's not that big of a job."

"OK. OK." Freddy, who was playing the part of Vance Stewart, paused. Then he said, "I might be able to help you."

"So what about it? Have you got a buddy or don't you? What I've got is a job for two."

"You're in luck, Mister. A buddy of mine is gonna meet me here at ten o'clock."

"That's swell." Roger paused. "I'll be over by the jukebox taking a look at the bubbles. If your buddy shows up and wants in on the deal, come see me." Roger switched back to his narrator voice. "After that I went to the jukebox. I kept one eye on the bubbles and one eye on Vance Stewart. At ten o'clock exactly a boy came in and sat down next to him. I recognized the boy from a photo Mrs. Berk had given me. It was Johnny Berk. He was wearing the same sort of leather jacket that Vance Stewart was wearing. The two boys began talking. I knew Vance Stewart was telling Johnny about my offer. Johnny began shaking his head. It looked like he was saying no to the deal. Then, Johnny abruptly stood up. He walked out of the bar without looking back. At that point I quickly made my way to the back of the bar. When I got to the back, I quietly opened the back door, stepped out into the alley, then ran up the gangway at the side of the bar until I reached the front. There I saw Johnny Berk half a block away. I began to follow him."

The story went on for another twenty minutes. The upshot of the story was that Johnny told Vance the next day that he was going home to see his mother in Chicago. That's why Vance sent a letter to Johnny in Chicago. The papers that Vance's girlfriend Judy sent him were test answers she'd stolen from her father, who was a professor. Vance and Johnny planned to sell the answers to her father's students. But in reality, Johnny was never in Chicago, because he and Judy had run away together. Eventually, Vance tracked them down and stabbed Johnny to death in a jealous rage. Ballard, of course, figured out what happened. So by the end, Vance heard the shadow's voice, just like all the killers do.

After the broadcast, I telephoned Minnie. I had no idea what hints were supposed to be hidden in the episode. I wanted Minnie to tell me about the clues she thought were there.

After she answered the call, she asked, "What did you think?"

"I don't know what to think," I said. "I couldn't make anything out of it related to Leonard's accident."

"To begin with, there's the fact that the story is about two boys who run off together," Minnie said. "That's what I think Leonard and Ray did."

"You think they left town together?"

"I do. And I think Gloria added a clue about where they went. Leonard and Gloria have a cottage in Saugatuck, Michigan that they use during the summer months. Leonard used to talk about his favorite bar there. It was a joint called Blondie's."

"So Gloria turned that into Blackie's?'"

"Right. And also Leonard told me why he liked Blondie's so much."

"OK. I'll bite. Why?"

"Because they have a Wurlitzer Bubbler jukebox that plays opera."

I whistled. "That pretty much nails it."

"Yes. And there's another thing. From what Leonard told me, Blondie's is a bar like the Dome."

"You mean a piano bar?"

"No, angel, I mean a bar where gentlemen sometimes meet other gentlemen. You see, Saugatuck is known for its bohemian citizens. They have a beach there, Oval Beach, which, according to Leonard, is, uh, a men's nude beach."

"Oh, really. I didn't know such a thing existed."

"According to Leonard, it does."

"That sounds intriguing."

"I've thought of visiting there myself," said Minnie. "But I don't think it would get me anywhere."

"Is that all?" I asked.

"Well, did I mention that Ray loves to smoke cigars? And that he wears a leather jacket and rides a motorcycle?"

"That can't be a coincidence," I said. "So, in Gloria's script, Vance is a stand-in for Ray?"

"I'd say so," Minnie agreed. "And Johnny is a stand-in for Leonard."

"Anything else?"

"There's one more thing." Minnie paused. "In real life, Leonard's mother owns a gift shop called 'Lehnerts.'"

"OK. And do they sell paperweights?"

"Probably."

"Wait. Don't tell me that Leonard used to drop off shady packages for money."

"No, nothing like that," Minnie said. "Gloria made that part up. Obviously she had to write the script to suit the characters in the show. That's how she works.

She draws ingredients for the characters in her scripts from real life, then mixes them into a made-up story."

"I suppose if she did it with 'The Fortune-Teller' episode, she might have done it with this one."

"There's another ingredient from Leonard's life that she used." Minnie said. "Both Leonard's and Ray's fathers died when they were young."

That was another piece of evidence that Minnie was right. "I see what you're saying," I said. "There are too many similarities for it to be a coincidence. But what can I do with it?"

Minnie was silent for a moment. Then she said, "Maybe you should drive out to Saugatuck and see if you can find them."

"I'd have to talk to Gloria first, wouldn't I?" I asked. "I'd need to get the address of their cottage."

"I don't think you should talk to Gloria. If she knew you were going there to look for Leonard and Ray, she'd call and warn them you're coming."

"Then how do I find them?"

"I think you should go to Blondie's. Someone at Blondie's is sure to recognize them. You have photographs of both of them that you can show."

"I don't know." The idea seemed like such a long shot. I wasn't sure how I could justify it. I said, "Driving to Saugatuck would cost a lot more than taking a cab to Gloria's apartment in Hyde Park."

"Do you have a car?"

"Vito does. He has an MG Roadster."

Minnie whistled into the receiver. "Fancy!"

"He inherited it."

"From who? His father?"

"Something like that. It's a long story."

"Will he let you borrow it?"

"Probably. He let me drive it once before."

When I hung up my call with Minnie I realized there was a lot I wasn't sure about. But some pieces of the puzzle were beginning to fall into place. The various fragments of the Lehnerts' case that had seemed all mixed-up were beginning to come together. The facts of the case were still a bit jumbled in my mind's eye. But then, as if I was looking at one of Gloria and Leonard's cubist paintings, I saw how the disassembled pieces of the puzzle, when looked at from a certain angle, could be viewed in such a way as to form an image. And I began to build in my mind a picture of what really had happened.

24

Vito's 1948 MG Roadster was a red convertible with tan leather seats. Like all MG Roadsters, the fins on the exterior front grill were painted to match the color of the interior upholstery. It was quite a put-together look, the kind of look that turned heads. When I first saw the car, I told Vito it looked like a pocketbook on wheels.

On my way to Saugatuck I drove the Roadster with the top down. I had to take off my hat, stow it in the passenger footwell, and cover it with my jacket to keep it from blowing onto the highway. Since I wasn't wearing my hat, by the time I parked near Blondie's bar on Culver Street in Saugatuck, my hair was more windswept than the prairie.

I flipped down the mirror on the back of the visor, then restored order to my hair using the Brylcreem I had stashed in the glove box. I put on my hat, hopped out of the car, and strode to the front door of Blondie's bar with confidence.

Above the entrance door was a large electric sign with the name 'Blondie's' in yellow neon script next to a white neon martini glass that held two green neon olives. Below that was a red neon arrow that helpfully pointed down to the front door.

I stepped inside to an interior dominated by a square-shaped mahogany bar that was built into the middle of the room. At the center of the square stood a tower of glass shelves that held bottles of liquor, all lit from below to show off their alluring colors. Tan upholstered stools sat around the four sides of the bar and around the perimeter of the room. Also along the walls were coffee-colored cocktail tables, fern-laden planters, and, sitting against the far wall, a sparkly and colorful jukebox.

To make sure I was in the right place, I went straight for the jukebox to see what it had to offer. The jukebox matched Gloria's script exactly. It was a Wurlitzer Bubbler with a selection of popular music and opera. I figured as long as I was there, I ought to play something.

Right away I saw what I wanted. I put in my nickel and chose a recording of Enrico Caruso singing "Vesti la giubba" from Leoncavallo's opera *Pagliacci*. It was one of Vito's favorite arias. According to Vito, the song comes at the end of the first act, when the stage performer Canio discovers his wife's infidelity, but despite this must prepare for his performance as Pagliaccio the clown. "The show must go on," Vito said. "No matter how much it hurts. The people pay you and they want their laugh." For Vito, the song was a reminder of what it felt like to be in the ring and take a fall—a swan dive, he called it—at the hands of "some cream puff" that Walt Winkler had bet on to win.

After I'd made my selection, I walked over to the bar and sat down. The bartender, whose name tag identified him as Tim, was nicely dressed in a white shirt with rolled-up sleeves and a shiny black tie that matched his curly black hair. He looked young enough to be the son of Walt, the bartender at The Dome. Tim had an adorable face that was made more appealing by a playful smile. I ordered a grasshopper. It was a creamy sort of drink, the kind of cocktail that would've made Vito roll his eyes. But I didn't care. I liked how it tasted.

Tim glanced at me sideways as he poured crème de menthe, crème de cacao, and cream into a cocktail shaker, then put the cap on the shaker. He rhythmically shook it from side to side and then up and down the way a musician might shake a maraca.

"That's quite a rhythm," I told him. "Your wrist action is dynamite."

Tim smiled. "Thanks!"

From the inside pocket of my jacket I pulled out the photo Minnie had lent me. It was the picture that George had taken on Ray's last night at The Dome. I held it out for Tim to see. "Maybe you can help me. I'm looking for a man named Ray MacDonald." I pointed at the man in the photo wearing a Hawaiian shirt. "Have you by any chance seen him here?"

"What do you want with him?"

"I'm trying to track him down, along with a friend of mine named Leonard, who has a summer cottage here. Leonard always says Blondie's is his favorite hangout." I took out the Tribune photo of Leonard and showed it to Tim. "This is a picture of Leonard."

Tim looked doubtful. "My boss is not too crazy about me giving out information about customers," he said. "Fellows like their privacy, you know what I mean?"

I nodded.

Tim stared at me. "How's your grasshopper?" he asked in a cordial tone.

"Creamy," I said. Then after a moment, I added, "And minty."

"Is that how you like it?"

"Yeah."

"Good." He leaned in on the bar and said, in a confidential manner, "You know some men think a grasshopper is a girlie drink."

"Do they?" I shrugged. "It doesn't bother me."

"I can see that," said Tim. "And in my book that makes you OK." He winked at me. "You know what I mean?"

"I'm not sure I do." I couldn't tell if he was making a pass or trying to decide if I was trustworthy.

Tim wiped a beer glass with a towel. Then he started on a wine glass. "Here's the thing. I figure a guy who orders a grasshopper has to be on the level. You know what I mean?"

I nodded. "I *am* on the level." I returned his wink. " … in every way."

"So I can see you're not some tough guy looking to screw anybody over." He glanced around.

"Then can you help me?"

"Things are a bit quiet right now," he said. "Maybe later tonight, like after ten o'clock, you might have better luck."

"After ten o'clock?"

"Yeah, that's generally when things get busier."

"OK. Thanks." I said.

"And by the way," said Tim, while casually buffing the surface of the bar with his towel. "I get off at 2:30 a.m. So in case you should be interested in a nightcap, I live a block away."

"Sounds convenient," I said. "I'll keep that in mind."

"I hope you do!"

I looked at my watch. It was only nine p.m. I was going to have to find a way to nurse my grasshopper for an hour. I held the cocktail glass up to my lips and tentatively licked a morsel of cream off the rim while Tim watched me. I was pretty pleased with myself. I had pulled off my mission the same way Percy Ballard would have done it. I'd gotten someone to trust me, not by being a tough guy, but by being the opposite.

Three new customers walked in and Tim got busy serving them. I picked up my drink and wandered back to the jukebox. Hearing Caruso's aria filled me with longing for Vito. I'd tried to talk him into coming with me to Saugatuck, but he told me he had too much studying to do. He was hopped-up about a new project Professor Arden was working on that had to do with Neptune's moon Triton. When he told me about his astronomy project, I slipped up and called him "a regular Dr. Zarkov." He laughed at first. But then a suspicious look came over him.

"Why'd you call me that?" he asked.

"I think you know," I said. I realized my mistake. But I figured if I could play it cool, he might not notice. "You know who he is, right? The egghead on Flash Gordon?"

"Yeah," Vito said. "I know who he is. You're not the first guy to call me that. Some of the guys on the submarine used to rib me about it, too."

"I guess they had your number even then."

Vito made a sour face. "I never thought it was that funny, to tell you the truth."

I'd thought about leveling with Vito right then. And I almost did. I was on the verge of saying it out loud. "I read your private letters. I know all about you and Freddy." But I couldn't do it.

Lying to him, even indirectly, was eating me up. I

didn't know which would turn out worse, keeping secrets from him, or telling him the truth. I could foresee a bad outcome no matter what I did. I knew I had to be honest. There was too much at stake. Sooner or later I was bound to let something slip that I couldn't gloss over. Now that I was by myself, a few hundred miles away in Saugatuck, listening to Caruso on a jukebox in a bar, I could convince myself that I'd tell Vito the truth as soon as I got home.

I turned around and saw Leonard Lehnert.

I could hardly believe it. I wanted to put down my cocktail glass and rub my eyes. It was definitely him. There was no doubt about it. He looked exactly like the photograph that had been published in the Tribune, except that the black and white newspaper picture didn't show the chestnut color of his hair, the emerald green of his eyes, or the deep tan of his skin.

He also looked like the body I'd seen in the morgue, except there were no bruises on his face, his hair wasn't disheveled, and his skin wasn't waterlogged.

He wore a brown and yellow checked shirt and a cream-colored sports jacket. His brown gabardine pants weren't as tight as a wrestling singlet, but tight enough to be almost as clingy and nearly as revealing.

I assumed he had just walked in. He stood at the bar with his thumbs in his pockets, looking around awkwardly. I didn't know if he was looking for someone in particular, or to see if anyone noticed him, or if he was simply surveying the bar.

After a moment, he pulled out a stool and took a seat next to the spot where I'd been sitting. I gulped down the last of my cocktail, then walked back to the bar and sat down next to him.

I couldn't decide what to do. Leonard didn't know me from Adam. I could easily watch him anonymously if I wanted to. But I'd told Tim the bartender that Leonard and I were friends. If I sat next to Leonard and didn't talk to him, Tim might be suspicious. Maybe that didn't matter. But I had to decide quickly, because I couldn't just sit there and pretend everything was normal.

"Leonard?" I said, turning to the man next to me. "I'm Elliot Blake."

Leonard Lehnert looked at me. "Do I know you?"

"I recognize you from your picture," I said. "In the paper."

"Oh, that!" Leonard smirked. "I never knew how many readers the Tribune had until they published that picture!"

"And I'm a fan," I said. "Of *The Shadow's Voice.*"

Leonard blinked. "Oh, right ... well ..." He looked around the room. "A lot of people mistake me for that actor on *The Shadow's Voice.* But I'm not him. I get it a lot, though."

"We have a mutual friend. I live with an old pal of yours: Vito Vellucci. Vito saw you on a streetcar on Clark Street not long ago."

"He must have seen the actor."

"You want another grasshopper?" This came from Tim, who was standing on the other side of the bar looking at me. I wasn't sure how long he'd been standing there.

"OK," I said gamely. I turned to Leonard. "Can I buy you a drink?"

Leonard looked at Tim, then back at me. "Sure. Why not?"

Tim turned to Leonard. "What can I get you?"

"I'll have a sidecar," Leonard said. "I'm just in the mood." He shook a cigarette out of a pack of Pall Malls.

Tim nodded. "One grasshopper, one sidecar, coming right up!"

"What brings you to Saugatuck?" Leonard asked. He took out a lighter, lit his Pall Mall, and blew smoke out through his nose. He still had no idea what was going on.

"I was hoping to find Ray MacDonald."

"What?" Leonard's eyes went wide. "Wait a minute. How do you know Ray MacDonald?"

"I heard about Ray from Minnie McNally."

"Minnie!" Leonard laughed and the smoke from his cigarette came out of his nose again. "Leave it to Minnie to spill the beans about me and Ray. But I won't say anything against her. Minnie is great!"

"I think she is, too," I said. "And what a singer."

"She is," Leonard agreed. "You've seen her show at the Dome Room?"

"I was there a couple of days ago," I said. "And while I was there I met her friends Walt and George …"

"George! Oh, God," said Leonard. "Poor George. He tries so hard!"

"I know," I said. "He tried with me."

"I believe that," said Leonard.

"Now, Leonard, I have to point out, you've just let it slip that you know Minnie, who is an actress on *The Shadow's Voice*. She knows you. You can't keep pretending that you're just someone who happens to look like Leonard Lehnert."

He was silent for a long moment while he studied my face. Then he said, "Oh, all right, I guess you've got me." He took a nervous drag on his cigarette, turned toward the bar to tap the ash into an ashtray, then turned back to face me with a sheepish look. "You see, sometimes fans can get a bit aggressive. They want autographs. They want to become my new best friend. So out of habit I automatically pretend I'm someone else."

"I can understand that."

"But getting back to Vito." He spoke as if he was his gossip columnist character from *The Shadow's Voice*, all chatty and friendly. "I haven't seen him since high school. You said you live with him?"

"I do. We're very close. You know what I mean?"

"I think I do. It seems we have something in common." Leonard thought about it. Then he tilted his head back, took a puff on his Pall Mall, and asked, in a slightly catty tone, "Have you met Freddy?"

"I know who he is. He's on your show."

"Yes. Yes, of course. But did Vito tell you anything about him?"

"Not exactly," I said. "But Minnie did."

"Oh, that Minnie!" Leonard waved his cigarette in the air. "It's a good thing the WACs refused to take her during the war. She's a security risk!"

"She seems to have the inside info about everyone."

"Including me, it seems," Leonard said in a weary tone. It was clear he was still trying to gauge how much I knew.

"One grasshopper. One sidecar," said Tim as he set our drinks in front of us. "One shot of tequila for me," he added. Then he poured and drank the shot.

"Timothy," said Leonard in a scolding voice. "What are you doing? You have a long night ahead of you."

"I do," Tim admitted. "That's why I'm having this shot."

Tim left and Leonard stubbed out his cigarette. "So what has Vito been up to since high school?"

"He's a professional boxer, at least some of the time."

"Oh, right." Leonard sipped his drink. "I think Freddy mentioned that. Who would have thought? Back in high school, Vito was interested in wrestling."

"So I've heard," I said.

"I suppose he's got the body for it," said Leonard.

"He also studies astrophysics."

"You're joking."

"I'm serious. He's a doctoral student at the University of Chicago."

"I always thought he was … you know … just an athlete."

I nodded. "A lot of people think that. But there's more to him than meets the eye."

"So now, wait a minute," said Leonard. "If you know Vito and Minnie and George, and you're looking for Ray … what exactly … what is it you want with me?" His tone was suddenly serious.

"I've been investigating your death," I said. "Or more specifically, the death claim that your wife Gloria filed with my company."

"What!"

"I'm the claims investigator at Amalgamated Home and Life."

"Oh, shit!" He stood up. "Excuse my French. But I feel like I've just heard the shadow's voice. I wouldn't have pegged you for a detective."

"I'm here because I have a theory about why you staged a phony death."

"You do?"

"The only thing I'm not sure about is who you got to play the role of the deceased. It must have been a difficult role to cast."

Leonard rolled his eyes. "Since the jig is up, so to speak, I may as well level with you. Finding a body was what set this whole thing in motion. That and Gloria's damn script." He looked at me anxiously. "I suppose now you're going to turn me in." He picked up his sidecar, took a big sip, then set it back on the bar.

"I don't know what I'm going to do," I said. "I'd like to understand more about what happened."

"Are you serious?" Leonard looked shocked. "You mean you might approve the claim, even with me being alive?"

"No," I said. "I definitely won't approve the claim. But denying your claim and turning you in for fraud are two different things."

"OK," he said quickly. "I can see that. Thank you for considering that." Leonard fingered the rim of his sidecar glass. "I guess if you're willing to think about overlooking the … uh … fraud, I'd better talk to you." He sat back down, picked up his glass, and swallowed the last of his drink. "What is it you want to know?" he asked. "I guess at this point I might as well tell you everything."

"You can start by telling me where you got the body that ended up in the morgue."

Leonard grimaced. "Like I said, the body is what set the whole thing in motion. It was a fluke, really," he said. "Ray found it. And it was just after we'd written 'The Fortune-Teller' script. But I don't want to talk about it here. Let's go somewhere private."

"Where do you want to go?"

"You could come to my summer cottage. That's

where Ray and I are staying. You can talk to Ray there. He can tell you himself what happened."

"OK."

Leonard shook his head. "Ray is not going to believe this. Now maybe he'll admit that what I've been telling him for weeks is true."

"What's that?"

"Playing dead is the worst role I've ever played."

25

Leonard and Gloria's summer cottage in the woods near Saugatuck was homey and more modest than their Hyde Park apartment. We walked in through the kitchen, past an ivory Frigidaire, a three-burner electric stove, and a pair of robin's egg blue cabinets over a sink. There was an old sofa in the screened-in living room. Across from the sofa were two worn chairs on either side of a small Westinghouse Bakelite radio that, I noticed, had a big dial that was set at 720 for WGN. Ray was sitting in one of the chairs.

Leonard introduced me to Ray, referring to me as the bloodhound who'd tracked them down.

"What have you told him?" Ray asked.

"I've told him I'm not dead, obviously," said Leonard. "But he's here because I said you could tell him about how you found the body."

Shock registered on Ray's face, but he quickly got

control of his emotions and smiled. "You have terrible manners, Lenny," said Ray, rising from his chair. He shook my hand. "Please excuse Leonard," he said. "It seems you've cornered us. He's not very nice when he's cornered. And believe me, I know. Please have a seat. Can I get you something?"

"No, thank you."

Ray MacDonald was well put-together. He was taller and heavier than Vito, though not quite as muscular. He was athletic and clean-cut with a square jaw. His brown hair was wavy, and so thick that it would never need a dab of Brylcreem. Based on what Minnie had told me, I was expecting him to be something of a he-man. But at home with Leonard, he was soft-spoken and had a gentle demeanor.

Ray sat back down. I took the other chair, and Leonard perched himself on the sofa. Leonard talked to Ray as if I wasn't there. "And get this," he said. "Elliot and Minnie figured out we were in Saugatuck by reading between the lines of Gloria's most recent script!"

"I'm not surprised," Ray said. "After listening to the show last night, I got the feeling that, whether she realized it or not, your wife was giving out little hints about us right and left."

"She didn't do it on purpose," said Leonard. "She just has a shocking scarcity of ideas."

Ray nodded. "I suppose you're right. And, really, it's hard to blame her. How many times have you told me that coming up with a brand-new story, week after week, is draining?"

"It must be tough to come up with new material," I offered.

"What was the main thing that gave us away?" asked Leonard.

"It was the jukebox at Blackie's with opera recordings," I said. "Minnie was the one who told me about Blondie's. She knew it was your favorite bar in Saugatuck. That was just too much to be a coincidence."

Leonard shook his head. "Laziness. Pure laziness. I mean she barely tried to hide anything in that script. She turned my Blondie's' into her Blackie's," he said. "How blatant is that? She could have easily come up with something less similar."

"Like what?" asked Ray.

"I would have told her to call the bar Figaro's," said Leonard. "That would have tied in the opera angle without pointing the spotlight on Blondie's."

"As I told Leonard earlier," I said, "I'd like to understand what happened. How did you end up in this situation?"

"Well, if you really want to go back to the beginning," Leonard said. "It goes back to the war."

"He's right," said Ray. "Our problems, and my specific problem that led to this situation, began during the war. I was in the Navy. I was stationed at Pearl Harbor."

"Actually," I said. "I already know that part of the story. You're talking about Father Whalen, right?"

"Yes, but how could you know that?" asked Leonard.

"Because Vito was at Pearl Harbor, too." I said. "And as it turns out, he had an incident with the chaplain, Father Whalen, too."

"Who's Vito?" asked Ray.

"Vito is Elliot's friend," said Leonard. "You know, sweetheart, just like you're my friend."

"Oh," said Ray.

"And I'm sure I've mentioned Vito to you somewhere along the line, Ray," Leonard added. "Vito and I went to high school together. He was on the wrestling team with me."

"Oh," said Ray, "that guy."

I continued my explanation. "During the course of my investigation I talked to everyone in the cast of *The Shadow's Voice*. After I got to know her, I told Minnie about Vito's experience with Father Whalen. And then she filled me in on what he did to Ray."

"We had to get away from that louse," said Leonard. "And it had to be in a way that would put an end to his dirty tricks once and for all. That's the only reason I did what I did."

"Well, what did you do, exactly?" I asked. "I know about the boat. Your wife put all that in the claim. You were out in the lake and got knocked over by the boom. Wasn't that risky, to stage it that way?"

"Not really," said Leonard. "The boom didn't really hit me. You see, we rehearsed it just like we do at the studio. I stood in a spot near the side of the boat facing the boom. Gloria yelled, 'coming about,' and then just as the boom started to swing toward me, I braced myself. But just before it hit me, I did a kind of backwards dive into the water. We knew that from where Carl was watching it would look like the boom hit me in the face."

"But then how did you disappear?"

"I swam away; that's all. I only had to swim about thirty yards. I stayed underwater as much as I could. It was dark. So even when I peeked above water no one could see me. Hell, I couldn't see them."

"Thirty yards? I thought Gloria said you were further out in the lake than that when this happened," I said.

"Oh, we were. But I only had to swim to the breakwater."

"That's what I thought!" I smiled. "I knew it." I was pleased with myself. "So how did you get back to shore? Did you walk on the rocks?"

"Oh, no," said Ray. "I picked him up. I'd rented a dinghy before the sailboats left the dock. I rowed out to the breakwater to wait. We had it all worked out in advance. There was no way I was going to let Lenny get caught short out in the middle of the lake!"

"Well, then, here's the main question. Where did you get the body?"

"It was my brother's body," said Leonard.

"And I was there when he died," said Ray.

"What? Where?"

"On Lower Michigan Avenue," said Ray. "On the bottom level of the Michigan Avenue bridge over the river."

"You see, my brother, Greg, was an alcoholic," said Leonard. "It started when he got back from the war. He'd been a sergeant in the army. His unit took part in the Allied invasion of Normandy. He watched five of his men get blown up on the beach. He was never the same after that. By the time he died, he was living, if you can call it that, at the Pacific Garden Mission."

"Lenny spent years trying to help his brother," said Ray. "But nothing he did made any difference."

"His drinking just kept getting worse and worse. I couldn't take it any more. I couldn't stand seeing him in the gutter. And I finally realized that there was nothing I could do to help him," said Leonard. "So I let him go. I lost touch with him."

"Lenny and Greg's parents are both dead," said Ray.

"My dad died when I was only six. My mom died a decade later," said Leonard.

"So Greg didn't have anyone except Lenny to turn to," said Ray. "They have no other family."

"And by then Greg had lost all of his friends," said Leonard. "He drove away anyone who cared about him."

"It's a terrible situation," said Ray. "I sometimes

brought vagrants in off the street to the Pacific Garden Mission. Unfortunately there are a lot of alcoholics there. Most of them are alone—at rock bottom."

"If I'd known how bad Greg was," said Leonard. "If I'd known he was at the end of his rope, maybe I could have done something. It's just that I'd stopped being in touch with him because I couldn't take it. Even so, I planned to check in on him at Christmas. I knew he slept at the Mission. I figured I could find him there."

"Anyway," Ray continued. "I was aware of Lenny's brother's situation. Since my beat is downtown, I kept an eye on him whenever I could. He and the other drunks from the Mission sometimes panhandled down on Lower Michigan or Lower Wacker. I guess when the weather was bad that location was better for them because it kept them out of the rain or snow. But it was a creepy place to panhandle. It's dark down there. You won't find that many regular people walking around down there. Those who do venture down there give the drunks a wide berth. I can't imagine they got too many handouts."

"The problem is," said Leonard, "Greg was terrified of cops. He'd been arrested quite a few times. He said he'd rather be in the gutter than in a jail."

"So even though I was keeping an eye on him," said Ray, "it was impossible for me to talk to him. If I tried to get close or approach him, he'd run away."

"Which is why he did what he did on the night in question," said Leonard.

"I was walking my beat on Michigan Avenue the way I always did. It was Saturday night, September 25th. When I got to the bridge, I went down to Lower Michigan at the northwest end of the bridge to walk the lower deck. Right away I saw a drunk sitting on the railing of the lower level with his back against one of the diagonal trusses that support the lower deck. He was singing in a loud voice, either because of or despite the fact that there was no one around. His voice was distorted, but it sounded like he was singing "White Christmas," you know, that Bing Crosby song that was popular during the war, which was puzzling since it was September. It was hard to tell exactly what he was singing because he was three sheets to the wind. Someone must have given him a buck. There was an empty bottle on the deck of the bridge just below his feet. I started to walk toward him to check up on him. I didn't know it was Greg at that point."

"And when Greg saw a cop coming toward him," Leonard interjected, "he panicked."

"I was about fifteen feet away from him when he saw me. He'd been singing and looking at the water. But then he turned and saw me and I guess I startled him. He stopped singing. He jerked into motion. It looked like he was trying to swivel his legs around on the railing so he could hop down to the sidewalk. But his pants caught on something and he lost his balance. His legs flew up and his arms flailed. He tried to catch hold of the railing and he got it tucked under his arms.

At that point, he was hanging on the railing, facing the deck with his legs dangling over the water. He held like that for maybe ten seconds. But he couldn't hold his weight. His arms gave out and he started to fall. He tried to catch the railing with his hands, but he missed. I heard him scream. It was a terrible thing. I couldn't reach him in time. He hit his face on the deck of the bridge and then he dropped down straight into the water."

"Jesus," I said.

Ray continued. "I tried to save him. I ran to the end of the bridge where they keep life preservers behind glass on a column below the bridge house. I broke the glass, grabbed the preserver, and threw it into the river. So then I ran to the stairs that go down from the bridge to the river's edge. At that point, I saw him. His body was just beginning to sink into the river about thirty feet from the life preserver. I yanked off my shoes and jumped into the water. First, I swam to the preserver, then I grabbed it and swam with it over to Greg. After a lot of flailing around with his body, I managed to turn him over so he was face up. I towed him to the river's edge as fast as I could. I found a mooring rope attached to a post on the riverbank that was hanging down to the water. I tied the rope to his hands, got out of the water, and then I used the rope to hoist him up and out of the river. I laid him out on the embankment. But he had no breath, no pulse." Ray shook his head. "There was nothing I could do."

"You did everything you could, sweetheart," Leonard said.

"At that point I finally got a good look at his face. That's when I realized who he was," said Ray. "I went up to a phone booth on Michigan Avenue to call the department so they could notify the medical examiner. But knowing it was Lenny's brother, I decided to call him first. As it turned out, that made all the difference."

"Because I immediately told Ray not to call the department," said Leonard. "I asked him to wait while I talked things over with Gloria, then call me back. I had an idea, and it wouldn't work if Ray called the department right away."

Ray said, "So I agreed to wait and call Leonard back an hour later."

"I spent the hour talking to Gloria about my plan," Leonard continued. "You've got to understand, we'd just finished writing the script for "The Fortune-Teller." We'd come up with this gimmick where Rose tried to fake her suicide using Madam Delilah's body. And the whole thing hinged on the fact that Madam Delilah just happened to look like an older version of Rose."

"Greg was younger than Leonard," Ray interjected, "but drinking had aged him. His face was bruised from where he'd hit the bottom of the bridge."

"I went over the options with Gloria," said Leonard. "We both knew what was at stake. If Whalen had his way, all my fans would find out I'm … well, I guess you know what I am. So I told Gloria my idea. I said we could just follow our own script. If I played it like Rose in 'The Fortune-Teller,' Whalen would think I was dead. That would put an end to his little extortion once and for all." Leonard grimaced. "Ray and I talked about moving to California. We could start over. We could get new jobs. Gloria would have the insurance money." He paused and looked at me with a guilty expression. "So together, Gloria and I cooked up this sailing accident scheme in which I would die but my brother's body would show up in my place. My brother was already dead. There was nothing more I could do for him. And I know it sounds cold, but I thought, well, maybe Greg could do something for me. And that was how I came to undertake my most difficult role: playing dead."

Ray picked it up from there. "So when I called Lenny back an hour later, he told me about the new script and the plan they'd come up with. And even though it was a risk, I couldn't see the harm in it. The poor man was already dead. And it was a way out of the extortion. So in the end, I agreed. We all agreed to do it … together."

I nodded. I knew the gist of what they did after that. But I wasn't sure of the details or how they got away with it. "How did you get your brother's body to turn up in the river a week after Leonard's accident?" I asked

"That was me again," said Ray. "I put the body in my

car—in my trunk—until we were sure that Leonard and Gloria could pull off the boating accident on Lake Michigan. We staged the accident the next day, on September 26th. It was Gloria's idea to wait a few days after that before we released the body. I'm not sure it was the best idea. She said she wanted to be sure no one raised any red flags before we committed to having a body turn up. I kept ice around the body in the trunk of my car so we could preserve it as long as possible. But after a week, I told her we had to act, that I couldn't keep it going any longer. So on the evening of Friday, October 1st, I recreated what actually happened the night Greg died. I waited until my next shift started and parked my car again on Lower Michigan. Then after midnight, when I was sure no one was around, I took the body out of my trunk and carried it down to the river and dropped it in the water. After a couple of minutes I jumped into the water and hoisted the body out, using a mooring rope just like I did the first time."

"Why bother putting the body in the water, then pulling it out right away?" I asked.

"I wanted my clothes to be wet when Detective Thompson and the medical examiner arrived to inspect the body. I wanted to be sure everything matched what I planned to put in my police report. My plan was to say in my report that I was patrolling on the bridge; I spotted the body; I dove in the river to pull it out and determined that the man was dead."

"How about the paper with Leonard's telephone

number?" I asked. "Did Greg really have that in his pocket or did you put it there?"

"I put it there," said Ray. "That was part of Leonard and Gloria's plan. They knew Thompson would call the number. When he called it would be Gloria who would answer. The plan was that she'd ask Thompson if it was possible that the body could be Leonard's body. They also figured it was plausible that either Leonard or Greg might have Leonard's telephone number in his pocket."

"You really planned things out," I said. "And you almost got away with it. I was ready to pay the claim."

"There's something I want to be clear about, Elliot," said Leonard. "We shouldn't have filed the insurance claim. It was wrong for us to do that. It meant cheating your company out of a lot of money. But Gloria was worried that if the cops thought I'd died and we didn't file an insurance claim, that would raise a red flag that would make them suspicious. So in the end, we did file the claim."

I nodded. "I've had cases like that, where the police ask whether or not a beneficiary has filed a claim. They don't like it when someone dies in questionable circumstances that involve a beneficiary, but the beneficiary doesn't file a claim. It makes them wonder if the beneficiary is trying to hide something, like a motive."

"How did you figure out the dead body wasn't me?" asked Leonard.

"A couple of things went against you," I said. "First of all, as I told you, Vito saw you on a streetcar on Clark Street the same day Gloria identified your body at the morgue."

"I saw him, too," said Leonard. "I don't know how he happened to spot me. I was one of a dozen people looking out the window on that streetcar. Why was he even looking at the streetcar?"

"For the same reason, apparently, that you were looking at pedestrians."

Leonard threw up his hands. "Well, I think it was a one in a million chance that he saw me. It was just rotten bad luck for me."

"What were you doing on the streetcar?"

"I was on my way back to Ray's apartment, which is where I was hiding out. That was the one and only time I went out in public. I just rode the streetcar. I didn't even go anywhere in particular," Leonard exclaimed.

"I told you you shouldn't go out," said Ray.

"It was the day after Ray put Greg's body back in the river. I was going stir crazy. I had to get some fresh air."

"And then because of that," I continued, "Vito was suspicious. So when no one was looking, he took a closer look at the body in the casket at the funeral. After that, he was quite sure it wasn't you."

"So it was all thanks to Vito," Leonard observed.

"Well, that and the opera jukebox. I don't know how I'd have found you otherwise."

"So what are you going to do?" asked Leonard.

"I'm not sure," I said. "It seems to me the person who's really to blame for all this is Father Whalen. The rest of you … well … I see how you were just trying to get out from under him. The way I figure it, unless I'm missing something, if I don't pay the claim, then it will turn out that nobody got hurt."

"That's generous of you to look at it that way," said Leonard. "But if you deny the claim, we're back to the same problem Gloria was worried about in the first place. Won't it look suspicious?"

"It would," I said. "Since everyone thinks you're dead."

"I'm telling you, it's been my worst role," said Leonard.

26

———

In staging Leonard's death, Leonard, Gloria, and Ray had followed a carefully choreographed script: from Leonard's make-believe sailing accident, to Ray's substitution of Greg's body for Leonard's, to Gloria's identification of that body as her husband's. Each of them had played their part convincingly.

But if I was going to deny the claim without raising suspicion, there'd have to be a new script: one that could explain everything that had happened in a reasonable way.

Leonard was still sitting on the sofa. Ray was still sitting in his chair. They were both looking at me, waiting for me to explain what would happen if I denied Gloria's insurance claim.

"Well, in a lot of ways, you've done a pretty good

job of playing dead," I said to Leonard. "But I've been thinking about what to do, and I have an idea. Maybe you need to rewrite the script."

"What do you mean?"

"I think there's a way for you to magically come back to life."

"How?"

"I'm not sure if it would work. But it would help if you claimed that you never heard Gloria warn you that she was coming about."

"I don't see how that helps," said Leonard.

"Well, you and Gloria are the writers," I said. "But I was thinking you could say that after you fell in the water you got disoriented. You'd confirm that you'd been drinking. That's already in the report the police got from Gloria. It was dark. You'd say that when you came up for air, you couldn't see any of the boats. So you swam to the breakwater for safety. You remembered getting knocked off the boat by the boom. But you didn't hear Gloria warn you she was planning to come about. You could say that you and Gloria had quarreled the night before. Maybe you could say on the day of the accident you were feeling angry towards each other, as couples sometimes do. As a result, while you clung to the rocks reviewing and reliving what happened, you began to wonder if Gloria had knocked you off the boat on purpose. Eventually, a stranger in a rowboat saw you at the breakwater and picked you up.

You were unwilling to go back to your boat if Gloria, in anger, had intentionally tried to hurt you. So you asked the stranger to take you to shore. And that's when you decided to take a train up to Saugatuck to lie low while you sorted things out."

"I don't think Gloria would be too keen on the idea that I ran away because I thought she might have tried to hurt me," said Leonard. "It paints an unflattering picture of her."

"But the point is," I said, "as you sat up here at the cottage thinking over what happened, you realized that your quarrel with Gloria had been nothing more than a petty disagreement. You came to the conclusion that you were being paranoid, that you weren't thinking straight. You realized that, of course, Gloria wouldn't have tried to hurt you. She couldn't have done it on purpose."

"OK." Leonard shrugged. "I suppose that's plausible. But Gloria still won't like it."

"She might like it better than being charged with fraud," I said.

"Hmmm," Leonard raised an eyebrow. "Point taken."

"Can you pull it off?"

"I can pull off everything you've said so far," Leonard said. "But how do I start the process of magically coming back to life?"

"It's only been two weeks since the accident. You can call Gloria tonight. Then you and she can be reunited. After that, everyone will realize it's all been a big misunderstanding."

"I don't think your explanation will stand up," said Leonard. "In fact I'm afraid that what you've come up with so far has more holes in it than a colander."

"What holes?"

"Well, first off, what about the coroner? What about the police detective? What do we say to them?"

"When they ask, Gloria can say that when she saw your brother's body at the morgue, she thought it was you," I said. "It was a natural mistake, given her state of mind. She thought you were dead. He looks like you. It was a drowned body. Of course, you'll have to tell the funeral people what happened, that it was Greg who they buried. They'll have to change the name on the paperwork. But after that, everyone comes out clean."

"Cleanish, Elliot. At best," said Leonard. "But there are other problems. It might be plausible that I ran away to Saugatuck to spite Gloria after we had an argument, but why would I keep Carl in the dark? I had no beef with him. Why would I leave *The Shadow's Voice* in the lurch like that, without any notice?"

"You didn't. You could say that right after the accident you sent Carl a note explaining that you were taking two weeks off. The note said you were sorry for the short notice, but something came up and you were confident that Freddy could fill in for you for a couple of weeks. In the note you'd ask Carl to let Gloria and the rest of the crew know you were taking a break. That would explain why you didn't call her directly to tell her where you are. Since you were angry with her, and weren't speaking to her, you wrote to Carl. Your note to Carl would have prevented the death claim, the funeral, all of it."

"I could say I sent such a note. But Carl would point out that he never got such a note."

"That's not your fault. You dropped the note in the mail. You can't help it if the post office never delivered it. In fact, you should write a note like that right now, and mail it from here as soon as possible."

"But then the postmark date will be wrong."

"Yes. But it's better if Carl gets a note like that after the fact than if he never gets one at all. You can say it must have gotten stuck in the bottom of the mailbox here in Saugatuck and the mail carrier just now picked it up. That's hardly your fault."

"Well … maybe. It's not great, but I suppose it's almost plausible," said Leonard.

"I don't think we're ever going to find a cover story that doesn't raise some eyebrows," I said.

"Very well. I'll send Carl a note. But there's still one more huge problem. And I don't know how to fix it. How do we explain Greg's death?" asked Leonard. "That's the biggest hole of all!"

"We probably don't have to worry about that, Lenny," said Ray. "In my experience, once the department learns that the body I found belonged to an alcoholic who lived at the Pacific Garden Mission, they aren't going to spend much time looking into what happened. I know Thompson, the investigating detective. He's not the type to waste time trying to build a case when there are no clues or witnesses and no physical evidence to clearly show a crime was committed."

"But what if Thompson thinks it's too much of a coincidence that Greg just happened to die at the same time I was reported dead?" Leonard asked.

"Actually, that's easy to explain," said Ray. "Thompson would figure that Greg went on a bender or committed suicide because he'd learned of your death. Don't forget, as far as Thompson knows from my report, I found Greg's body three days after the accident. If I didn't know what really happened, I'd think suicide was the most likely explanation. You were Greg's only living relative. He had no other friends. Greg would have been devastated if he thought you'd died."

"But then what about Father Whalen?" asked Leonard. "We'd be right back where we started. Once he finds out I'm still alive, he'll go back to the extortion scheme."

"You don't have to worry about that either," I said. "When Vito found out what Father Whalen had done to you, he went to his church and had it out with him."

"Really?"

"Yes. I was there. You should've seen it. Vito laid him out with an uppercut punch. He knocked him right onto the pews. He made Whalen promise he'd never again do what he did to you. Otherwise, Vito told him, we'd reveal everything to the church authorities."

"I suppose we could have done that, too," said Ray. "I just pictured it as mutual destruction. We'd report him and he'd still ruin our lives."

"I think getting punched rearranged his thoughts about that," I said.

"To tell you the truth, it would be nice to have my old job back," said Leonard. "Roger won't be too happy about it. But this business with him and Freddy sharing my role--what idiot came up with that idea?"

"Carl told me he was desperate, because Freddy could only do the dandy part of the character," I said sheepishly.

"Oh, so you know Carl, too?" asked Leonard.

"I know everyone involved in this story," I said.

"Well I'm certainly ready to go back to work," said Ray.

"And then we'll have to bid adieu to Saugatuck," said Leonard. "I'll miss it —especially the jukebox at Blondie's."

"It will be nice to have you back on *The Shadow's Voice*," I said. "Roger and Freddy are pretty good. But they're not as good as you."

"Why, thank you!" said Leonard. "Maybe you and

Vito and Ray and I can all get together to catch Minnie's act at the Dome Room one of these days. I want to thank her personally for spilling the beans on me and Ray and Father Whalen."

"She'll be glad to find out you're alive," I said.

27

———

When I got back home late Sunday night, I was in a chipper mood. I couldn't wait to tell Vito how I had solved the case—how everything was going to work out beautifully for everyone involved. I found Vito waiting for me. I had barely walked in the front door when he confronted me.

"Is there something you want to tell me, Elliot?"

"What are you talking about?"

"I'm talking about my private letters. They're in a box in the back of the closet. I had them organized a certain way. And today when I looked at them, I found out that somehow they had become disorganized. And I want to know how."

"OK," I said. "I was planning to say something to you about that."

"What did you do?"

"I was in the closet and I found the box."

"And you opened it? Even though you knew it was private?"

I nodded. "I'm sorry, Vito."

"Why? Why would you do that?"

"It was the morning after the funeral. I was jealous. I was crazy jealous. I'm sorry. I know it's the one thing you don't want me to be. I just couldn't help it."

"Jealous? Jealous of who?"

"Of Freddy."

"Freddy! What does Freddy have to do with it?"

"We'd just seen him at the funeral. Before that I didn't know anything about him. But it was obvious you and he had been in a relationship. And then I thought maybe when you saw him again ... I thought maybe it might reawaken things between you."

"I don't believe this."

"And when I asked you about him, you said your life was an open book. So I ... I thought reading some of your old letters was just, you know, in keeping with that idea that your life is an open book."

"Elliot, you read my letters?"

I nodded.

"My fucking private letters!"

"Yes. I'm sorry."

"And now you're telling me it's because I said my life is an open book?"

"I know it's not a good excuse. I was wrong to do it."

"Why? Why did you have to do that? Do you know

how it makes me feel? Jesus, Elliot." Without warning, Vito began to cry.

"I'm sorry."

"You …. you … why do I always end up in this situation? You'd think I could meet someone, just once, someone with a modicum of self-worth."

"I'm so sorry."

He began pacing back and forth. He clenched his fists. "Get out! I can't be around you right now." He pounded his right fist three times into the back of the sofa.

"What? Where am I supposed to go? I don't know where to go."

"Figure out something. As far as I know, this is still my house. And I want you out!"

"OK," I said. "I'll go. Maybe I can go to Maurice's."

"Fine. Just go! Go before I do something I regret!" He stared at me menacingly, with his fist clenched in the air.

I turned to leave. "Before I go, I have to run upstairs," I said. "I need to pack a few things to take with me."

"Hurry up! Hurry up! Or I swear to God!"

I ran up the stairs. My heart was racing. I haphazardly pulled two pairs of pants and two shirts out of the closet. I grabbed two pairs of socks and underwear out of the dresser. I found a shopping bag on the floor of the closet and stuffed my clothes into it. I ran down the stairs. I grabbed my coat and hat from the coat rack next to the front door.

I'd have to telephone Maurice. I couldn't just show up at his door unannounced. I thought about using the telephone in the house. But I was afraid if I didn't leave right away, Vito might do something crazy. I decided it would be better if I went to a phone booth.

I opened the front door and turned to look back into the house. Vito had collapsed onto the sofa in the living room. His eyes were closed. His cheeks were wet with tears. I closed the front door and began to walk down the front stairs. The significance of what was happening was just beginning to sink in. All of a sudden, I was crying, too. A deep wrenching pain clutched my heart.

What had I done?

28

Maurice was a set designer for the Goodman Theater. The job had come to him by chance when his predecessor had died unexpectedly during a production of *Lady Windermere's Fan*. The general manager of the theater had turned to Maurice because of Maurice's familiarity with the works of Oscar Wilde, who had written the play. According to Maurice, the manager had a crush on the actor Ronald Coleman, who'd played Lord Darlington in the 1925 silent film of the play, and whom Maurice, in Maurice's opinion, strongly resembled. Maurice did such a good job with *Lady Windermere*, he was offered a permanent position.

Maurice lived in a top-floor studio apartment just north of the river that bore a resemblance to an artist's garret. It was lit by three north-facing windows that slanted inward from the ceiling down to the sill and

269

overlooked the rooftops of the buildings nearby. Everything in his studio was either black or white. Black and white ceramic tiles covered the floor. The living area was furnished with a white sofa, a white chaise lounge, two black leather chairs and a black coffee table. The only color in the room came from the bright yellow decorative pillows he'd positioned on the sofa, and from the yellow roses that sat in a white vase on the black coffee table.

Maurice himself habitually dressed in black and white, almost always with his signature dash of color, which, depending on his mood, would show up in his tie or his pocket handkerchief or his hat or, if he was being subtle, his socks. He had thick but unruly dark hair, a mustache that he trimmed to be pencil-thin, and a fussy manner, though in private he would sometimes, as he put it, let his guard down.

I was perpetually amazed that he'd chosen me to be his best friend. We met in high school, where from the moment we met he behaved as though he were infatuated with me, despite the fact that I was out of his league when it came to intellect and taste. Nothing romantic had ever happened between us, although there was one awkward time when he'd put his arms around my waist and peered intently into my eyes, and I'd pulled away in embarrassment. Then he'd made some remark that was meant to be a wisecrack, but sounded menacingly vicious.

I wasn't sure that Maurice was the best person to go

to for comfort. He had a barbed tongue. He took pride in being an unsparing observer who would gleefully berate any dimwit who dared to cross him. Every biting word in my vocabulary was a word I had learned from him. But when confronted with the facts of my falling out with Vito, he was transformed. He became the sweetest, kindest fellow you could imagine. He handled my agony with kid gloves.

"Give him time," Maurice said.

"It's too late," I whined. "I ruined everything."

"You betrayed his trust. He's hurt. But he'll soften up."

"Why couldn't I have just trusted him?"

"In the scheme of things, the two of you haven't been together all that long. It takes time to build trust."

"I've known him long enough to know I shouldn't have read his private letters. But I did it anyway. It's because of my jealousy. He hates it when I'm jealous. It's the same thing that happened with him and Freddy. He broke up with Freddy because Freddy was too clingy."

"Are you sure it was that?"

"That's what he said."

"I thought you said it had to do with Freddy writing provocative letters that got Vito into hot water in the Navy."

"Well, there was that, too."

"Now, Elly, what you did isn't as bad as all that. You haven't gotten him into hot water."

"Maybe not. But I betrayed him. He's spent his whole life being betrayed by the people he loves."

Maurice threw up his hands. "Oh, Lord. I guess you're right." He pointed an accusing finger at me. "You snooped and spied shamelessly. Why you're no better than a peeping Tom the way you pried into his personal correspondence. He'll probably never want to see you again. I'll bet he's telephoned Freddy by now to ask him to come over."

"You think he'll call Freddy?"

Maurice glared at me. But then his expression softened into a smile. "No. I'm just tormenting you because you're such a sorry little puppy. I told you. Give him time. He'll come around."

"What if he doesn't?"

"Well, if Vito dumps you …" Maurice arched one of his eyebrows. " … I suppose we'll just have to go to the Dome Room for a nice drink and then maybe you can get something going on with George."

"George! Oh, Maurice. You really know how to hurt a guy."

"What's the problem? George, I'm told, is a very good accountant. He's quite nice. He has a lovely wife. And, of course, he has that cute polka-dotted bow tie!"

"Oh, God."

"And if it doesn't work out for you with George, then from what you've told me, there are plenty of other candidates who are ready to go for you in a big way. Let's see ... There's Walt at the Dome Room. There's, I think you said his name was Tim, at Blondie's, although that's in Saugatuck, so never mind about that. Then there's that very dapper chap at Marshall Fields you told me about. Mr. Geiger, I think you called him. I believe he was the one who helped you pick out your baby blue suit."

"Oh, Christ. Maurice! I told you, he did not help me pick it out. He trespassed all over my legs with his tape measure!"

"And then there's always little old me. You know I love you."

"Yes. Yes, I know."

"So?"

"So I'm not ready to think about anyone else. I love Vito. I really do."

Maurice sighed. "I know you do, pet. And that's why you just have to settle down, buck up, and muster some patience. Get a hold of yourself."

"I can't."

"Look. You love him and everyone knows it. You know you love him. I know you love him. And Vito knows you love him. In the end, that's all that counts."

"But what about Freddy?"

"What about him?"

"He's very handsome."

"Pfft. I don't know anything about Freddy. I've never met him. Though from your description it sounds like maybe I ought to. In any event, I strongly doubt he's as … how shall I put it? … as tasty-looking as you."

"You think that's all Vito sees in me … that I'm tasty-looking?"

"Don't knock it. But you have other desirable qualities."

"Like what?"

"Are you really going to make me do this? Are you going to force me to flatter you?"

"I could use it."

"Well … all right, Elly, let's see …, you're very clever at your job. I mean, from what you've told me, you just solved this *Shadow's Voice* business with practically nothing to go on except drive and determination."

"I did, didn't I?"

"Yes. And … uh … you have an excellent sense of style when it comes to clothes, which I imagine comes from your having studied at the feet of the master." He fanned his knuckles across his chest. "And you're loyal, reliable, and sweet. You're kind of charming, really. You're not dumb. You have a very pleasant way of smiling. You cross your legs nicely when you sit."

"You think that's a plus?"

"It is in my book."

"What about Vito?"

"Well … as far as Vito goes … I think you ought to make the most of that tasty-looking quality I mentioned. I know he likes to ogle you from behind. So the next time you see him, be sure to wear those pleated, grey-striped pants I bought you. The stripes are very effective in emphasizing what you've got going on back there."

"Maurice, I can't win him back that way. He's not that shallow. I have to find a way to rebuild trust."

"OK, then, why don't you write him a letter?"

"A letter?"

"Well, it seems to me that letter *reading* is what got you into trouble. Maybe letter *writing* can get you out of it."

"What should I say?"

"Just tell him how you feel about him. Didn't you tell me that he ate it up when you told him how much you loved him?"

"That's true."

"And then go through a list of things you like about him, the way I just did for you. Only don't mention his body."

"Why not?"

"For the same reason you kept asking me just now if there's more to you than your good looks. Apparently good-looking men aren't content to just be good-looking. You all want more. It's exhausting."

"All right, Maurice. I'll try writing him a letter."

"Good."

"But then I have to wait until it arrives. And then what? Do I call him? Do I visit him?"

"I don't know. But I suggest you slip the letter under his front door. This is no time to wait on the post office. And tell him in the letter that you plan to telephone him the next day."

"What if he doesn't answer my call?"

"There's no guarantee what will happen."

"I suppose not."

"Just remember, pet. You can always go to the Dome Room and sit at stool number five next to George on stool number six!"

I shook my head fiercely. "If Vito doesn't answer my call, I'm going to give up on men. I'll go back to Margo."

"Yes. That sounds like an excellent plan. I'm sure Margo will be thrilled to have you back."

"Really?"

"Elliot, look at me. Do I look like I'm serious? The odds of you giving up on men are about as good as the odds of me wearing denim jeans."

"I've never seen you in jeans."

"No. And you never will! They're blue!"

29

———————

I spent the next two hours writing my letter. I wrote some things that were apologetic, some things that were syrupy, some things that were angry, some things that were sexy, some things that I hoped were funny. But then I crossed all that out. When there were too many cross-outs, I crumpled up the paper and started over. Finally, after many attempts, I settled on what to say. I copied the final letter onto a new sheet of paper and showed it to Maurice.

He said, "That's fine. It's honest."

I said, "No edits?"

He said, "You're not writing a novel, darling. It's a letter. It's from *you*. You really don't want him to think you had help writing it, do you?"

"I suppose not."

"Then go with what you've got!"

.   .   .

HERE IS WHAT I WROTE:

Dear Vito,

I'm staying with Maurice for now. He suggested that I
write you a letter, which I thought was a good idea.
Writing this letter (and then rewriting it a few times)
has helped me understand why a letter should be kept
private. I've had to dig into my most personal feelings
to express what feels inexpressible. Doing that has
left me feeling exposed. If someone were to read what
I've written without my knowledge or permission, it
would feel as if someone spied on me while I was
naked.

I've thought a lot about why I'm so jealous all the
time, and why I have so little faith in myself. It has to
do with the way I felt growing up. When I was a kid, I
thought I was the only one in the world who didn't fit
in. I was uncoordinated, gangly, and not very smart. I
was painfully shy. I had a bad case of acne, which
made me feel ugly. My voice was high and squeaky. I
felt like a sissy, because I was.

Some of those conditions improved as I got
older. My voice got deeper. My skin cleared up. I
learned how to be more sociable, though I was only
able to do that with girls. Girls liked me, and that
was nice. But it didn't do anything for what I

secretly wanted. The other boys still thought of me as a wimp.

But the truth is, now that I'm grown up, I have nothing to complain about. I have a great job. I've had the immense happiness of living with the most wonderful man I could ever hope to meet. You've never once given me cause to be jealous. And yet I keep coming up with reasons to wallow in my insecurities.

I know I violated your privacy. It came out of jealousy, but it wasn't all jealousy. There's also a part of me that sincerely wants to know you as intimately as I can. That desire grows out of my love for you. You have such a unique mixture of qualities. You're brilliant, funny, thoughtful, forgiving. You're patient, though you can also burn hot. You're like an opera, an opera in the flesh: full of emotions, beautiful harmonies, roaring drama, and tender melodies. I never tire of getting to know you better.

I guess it goes without saying that I have practically no experience when it comes to romantic relationships. What little experience I've had was with Margo, and that was only useful in teaching me how to pretend to be something I'm not. What I want to do now is to learn how to be myself, to be honest about how I feel, and to not be ashamed. Can you help me grow and learn? Maybe I don't have the right to ask you. But I could never live with myself if I didn't try to win another chance with you. You are the most important person in my life. I ask you to forgive me. I promise that I will always try to respect your privacy, rise above my insecurities, and give you the freedom to be yourself without any pressure from me.

Please give me another chance.

I love you.

Elliot

30

———

I delivered the letter the next day. I spent all of my lunch hour on Tuesday making the delivery. Weeks ago I had traveled to Vito's house using the pretense of selling him an insurance policy. Now, again, I left work, took the elevated train up to the Bryn Mawr stop, walked to Vito's house on Magnolia street, climbed the porch steps, and stopped in front of Vito's door. I knew his schedule well enough to know that he was, or should be, in class. Even so, after I slid the letter under the door, I stood and stared at the piece of the envelope that remained visible on my side of the threshold, hoping that by some chance he'd come to the door and pick it up. I listened for the sounds of movement inside the house. There were no sounds. The letter lay still.

Finally, I turned, left the porch, walked back to the train, and rode it back downtown to my office. I was so anxious, I could barely concentrate on work. For the rest of the day, I glanced at the clock over and over again, watching the minute hand creep and the hour hand crawl. Finally, at five o'clock I left work to walk to Maurice's apartment on the north side of the river. Along the way, I walked by Marshall Fields on State Street. I saw a new suit in the display window. The baby-blue flannel suit was gone. The new one was a flecked tweed grey suit. It looked identical to the one Freddy had worn at Leonard's funeral. I tried not to read anything into it. But I felt an ache in my chest nevertheless.

When I got to Maurice's apartment, he asked me when I'd told Vito to expect my telephone call. It was only then that I realized I'd forgotten to add a p.s. in my letter to inform Vito that I'd telephone him the following day. That meant there was no timetable for what might happen next.

Maurice was clearly annoyed that I hadn't taken his suggestion. "That's why I told you to write in your letter that you'd telephone him at a specific time," he said. "Now you're just going to have to sit here and die a thousand deaths while you wait."

"What should I do?"

Maurice paced around the room, which was a habit of his when he was thinking. Then he said, "I made a joke earlier about taking you to the Dome Room. But I really do think that's what we should do. It's Tuesday night. Minnie's show is tonight. I think we should go there. You need something to distract you. You can tell Minnie all about how you solved *The Shadow's Voice* case."

"Yes," I nodded. "I suppose you're right."

"Good, then that's settled. Now I'll have to go to my room and select my ensemble."

We made plans to head to the Dome Room in time for Minnie's seven p.m. set. After rummaging in his closet, Maurice settled on wearing a black sport coat with black pants, and a white shirt with a white tie. The requisite touch of color came in the form of a pink handkerchief with small white polka dots.

"Look," he told me, as we got dressed. "I found the perfect hankie to wear in honor of George."

"What's the story between you and George?" I asked "Have you ever …?"

"No, no," Maurice said, "nothing like that. There may have been a moment early on … I guess it would have been when we first saw each other at the Dome that we briefly contemplated a flirtation. But the moment passed. Neither of us acted. And now, well … it's impossible! We've known each other for two years. It feels wrong to even think of him in that way."

Maurice and I arrived at the Dome Room at twenty minutes before seven. We took a seat at a table in the back. Almost as soon as we sat down, Minnie spotted us. She cast a knowing nod in our direction.

Then she turned and nodded at someone else. That someone else turned out to be Freddy, who was sitting on one of the stools near the front of the stage.

"Don't look now," I said to Maurice. "Freddy is here."

"What?" Maurice began to search the room. "Where? Where is he?"

"Over there," I pointed. "He's on stool number two. He's wearing the same flecked tweed suit he wore to Leonard's funeral. That also happens to be the suit that's in the window at Fields right now."

"Oh," Maurice exclaimed. I watched as his eyes landed on Freddy. "I've never seen him in here before."

"That's odd. I'm sure he comes here from time to time," I said. "Minnie is his best friend. They work together on *The Shadow's Voice.*"

"Well, well, well," Maurice sighed. "I had no idea."

"No idea about what?"

"That this fellow you've been telling me about would turn out to be so …"

"So what?"

"So very … I don't know …"

"Judging from your eyes, I think the word you're looking for is tasty."

"He's beyond tasty!" Maurice exclaimed. "He's … he's … a dreamboat!"

"Thanks, very much."

"Now don't be tiresome, Elly. Think of how good it is for you that I like him."

"How is that good?"

"Because in two minutes I'm going to go over there and flirt with him. And if by some miracle it turns out that he likes me back, then I believe all your troubles will be over."

"How so?"

"Obviously, once he falls in love with me, he'll forget all about your boxer friend."

"Maybe you can ask him if he's heard from Vito recently?"

"Are you crazy? I'm not going to do that," Maurice said. "You told me he's still mooning over Vito. Why would I mention him?"

"I suppose you're right."

"As a matter of fact," Maurice continued. "I'm going to act like I don't know you or Vito. I'm not going into this battle with one hand tied behind my back."

"Fine. Fine," I said. "Go to battle. But you'd better get going if you want to have time to talk before Minnie starts singing. Go and Godspeed."

'Wait! Where's George?"

I looked around the room. "I don't see him," I said. "He's not on his stool anyway. What does that matter?"

"I can't do this if George is watching. He'll laugh at me."

"Don't worry. He's not here."

"And come to think of it, would you mind very much? Could you go visit the men's room for a few minutes?"

"What?"

"I don't want you watching me either. It makes me nervous. I have performance anxiety."

"Oh, for God's sake, Maurice!"

"Please."

"OK."

I shook my head and left for the washroom. I stayed in the men's room for six minutes. It seemed like a long time. I thought six minutes ought to be long enough for Maurice to take a position and begin his attack. I pushed on the men's room door and tentatively peeked out. I could only see Maurice from behind. He was sitting on stool number three facing Freddy who was still on stool number two. From what I could tell from across the room, the situation looked promising. Freddy was smiling. Maurice, who can stiffen up when he's nervous, was talking and gesturing in an animated way. Minnie, who you would think would be focused on getting ready for her performance, was watching them. Then, as if she knew everything that was happening, she turned and looked directly at me. She raised an eyebrow.

I shrugged.

For the next ten minutes, Maurice and Freddy talked. They continued sitting together throughout Minnie's entire first set. Even after her set, when Minnie made her way down from the stage and came to sit with me, Maurice and Freddy remained in their seats on stools two and three, where they continued talking gaily.

"What's going on?" Minnie asked me.

"It's the invasion of Normandy," I said. "My friend Maurice has landed on the beach. Freddy is under assault."

"So I can see." She looked at me. "Somehow I didn't know that you and Maurice were friends. It figures. It's a small world around here. Did Maurice come with you?"

"Yes."

Minnie frowned. "But you promised me you were going to bring Vito for a visit? What gives?"

I hung my head. "Vito and I are having problems. I had to move out. I'm staying at Maurice's place now. It's a long story."

Walt, with his usual impeccable timing, arrived at that moment with drinks for both of us, which Minnie had ordered in advance. Minnie picked up her glass. "Well, here's to you. I've got thirty minutes before my next set. If it's such a long story, you'd better get started."

It took the entire thirty minutes and another round of cocktails for me to finish telling Minnie my version of the story. I started by telling her everything about my trip to Saugatuck and the miraculous resurrection of Leonard Lehnert, which she had already heard about, it turned out, from Ray, who'd stopped in briefly to announce that he'd be coming back to work next Friday.

Ray, in his recounting to Minnie of what happened, had described it as having all been a misunderstanding that had now blown over. He added a crucial bit of news, which was that Detective Thompson, upon hearing from Ray that the one-time victim of the boating accident, Leonard Lehnert, was still alive, but his bridge-jumping alcoholic brother was dead, had opened the police case file, scratched out a few words, written a few new words in their place, closed the file, shrugged, and said, "Well, that's that!"

Minnie, who knew the real story of what happened, was in awe of how well the cover story had gone over. "I gotta hand it to you," she said. "It was big of you to let the Lehnerts slide, given the false insurance claim."

I shrugged. "The only person at my office who knew about the claim besides me was Peggy, my secretary. I never got around to telling my boss about it. So I was able to handle the paperwork in my case file pretty much the same way Thompson did."

Minnie nodded. "You did the right thing. It was the damn priest who caused all the trouble. But what's all this about you and Vito?"

I had to wait until Minnie finished her second set before I had enough time to explain that.

31

The next day was Wednesday. It was another work day in which observing the minute and hour hands on the clock in my office became my sole preoccupation. By the time I left work and arrived at Maurice's apartment, I was full of despair. It had been more than 48 hours since I'd dropped off my letter at Vito's house. It had been more than enough time for him to have found it, read it, and come to a decision about what to do.

Maurice, owing to the great success of his debut encounter with Freddy at the Dome Room the night before, was as bubbly as I was listless.

He greeted me by saying, "Guess what! I have a surprise."

"Is it a good surprise?"

"Oh, yes. It's a very good surprise. I had a telephone call this morning from a Mr. Herbert Hauser in New

York City. Mr. Hauser is a theatrical producer. He saw my designs for Lady Windermere's Fan at the Goodman last year. And, well …" At this point, Maurice curtsied. "… he wants me to design a new production of that very same play for him."

"A production in New York?"

"Yes! Isn't that marvelous!"

"Congratulations, Maurice. That's very exciting for you."

"And there's more. I'm to go meet him this weekend. In fact I've already procured a ticket on the 20th Century Limited. I leave Saturday afternoon. I'll be in New York on Sunday morning."

"That's so sudden. You must be thrilled." I tried to sound happy for him, though my tone was not as enthusiastic as it might have been. I asked, "Will it be OK if I stay here while you're gone? I still haven't heard from Vito."

"Of course, Elly! You're welcome to stay as long as you need to."

"Thank you."

"I only have one favor to ask of you."

"What's that?"

"Will you come to the train with me on Saturday and see me off?"

"Do you need help with your luggage or something?"

"Now that you mention it, I will have to work up an assortment of outfits to wear. But, no, that's not the reason. You see, I've always had a particular fantasy. In my fantasy I'm sitting on the 20th Century Limited looking out the window just before the train leaves the station. The whistle blows, the cars lurch forward, and outside the window my friend is on the platform waving good-bye. I think I saw it in a movie once. It's very romantic."

"That's your fantasy?"

"Well, yes. It's like a bon voyage event—you know—like one of those scenes when the ocean liner leaves the port and everyone's waving good-bye, only this is when the train is leaving the station, which is almost as good."

"Fine." I shrugged. "If that's what you want, I'll come with you. What time does the train leave?"

"I leave from LaSalle Street Station at 3:00 p.m. Then, I arrive at Grand Central Station in New York at 8:00 a.m. Sunday morning. Then I'm meeting Mr. Hauser for lunch at Sardi's at noon."

"Sardi's?"

"Yes. It's a famous showbiz restaurant. Lunch at Sardi's is another fantasy of mine."

"It seems you're full of fantasies coming true."

"I am." Maurice beamed. Then he took a seat on the sofa next to me. "Now, Elly, I know you're feeling terribly forlorn at the moment. I know things don't look very bright right now."

"Are you kidding? My life is over."

"Well. Perhaps. But you don't know that yet. It's

only been a couple of days. He's Italian. Italians are very emotional. They burn hot. It may take a few days for him to cool down."

"Even after my letter?"

"It was a very nice letter, Elly. But we don't know what's going on, do we? Why, for all we know, he might have seen the envelope and decided not to even open the letter. People who are upset do crazy things like that."

"You think he didn't open it?"

"It's possible. My point is, we don't know what's what right now. So you have to be patient."

"I can't be."

"You need to be distracted. How about if we go out again tonight? I want to celebrate."

"You go," I said. "I'm just going to stay here."

Maurice shook his head. "OK. I suppose there's nothing I can do to cheer you up."

"No."

"Then I'm going to go get ready. I feel like wearing extra colors tonight."

So Maurice went out. I stayed on his sofa pretending to read a book while wrapped up in an afghan that Maurice's sister had crocheted. I was barefoot and my toes kept sticking up through the holes in the weave. In my mind I imagined Vito playfully pinching each toe as it popped out. This was what I'd come to.

Thursday came and went much the same as Wednesday had. I went to work. I came home. I had no word from Vito.

Then Friday came and went as well.

And still nothing changed.

By that point I felt like I couldn't take it any longer. More than anything I wanted to telephone Vito or go to his house. But Maurice insisted that I wait. Maurice was very firm. He said nothing could be worse than pushing a man when he clearly did not like being pushed. Maurice assured me that if only I could be patient, the volcano of passion would erupt again—as he put it.

"In eros veritas, Elly," he said, "in eros veritas!"

"What does that mean?"

"It is my belief," said Maurice, adopting a serious tone, "that eros is unerring in guiding us to our destiny. How else would two people who are so different come together with such passion?"

"Do you think Vito and I are so very different?"

"Yes. I do. But it's not just you and Vito, Elly. Look at most of the couples in the world. Most of the ones I know are as different as night and day. Only something as powerful as eros could have drawn them together."

"I guess if you put it that way," I said, "it's certainly true that men and women are inherently different."

"I'm not talking about gender, or opposites attract.

For some people, that kind of difference is enough, and maybe it's a lot. But there are many kinds of differences, Elly. We need people who expand us, who fill in what's missing, who push us where we wouldn't otherwise go."

"I can see how Vito does those things for me," I said. "But how do I expand Vito?"

"Well, you love him," Maurice said. "That's a start. Maybe that's what he needs most. Maybe that's what he's been missing. I'm not pretending I understand it all. But I am certain that our sexual organs are divining rods. They locate what we need!"

"OK, Maurice," I said. "I hope you're right. Because if there's no veritas in eros, I'm going to have to find the veritas in vino instead."

"Fine."

FINALLY, IT WAS SATURDAY, AND MAURICE WAS IN A frantic state of excitement. While getting ready for his journey, he managed to fill a trunk that was more suitable for an ocean voyage than it was for a four-day trip. I decided to help him slim down his baggage by physically repacking his clothes in a more modest-sized suitcase.

And then he surprised me by accepting my revamping of his luggage, perhaps as a concession to my mental state, although he did then ask if I would carry his suitcase for him at the station, since my doing so would help him with another detail of his bon voyage fantasy.

"My vision," he said, "is to walk down the platform while wearing a red scarf and smoking a cigarette in a cigarette holder. I can't really pull off the effect I have in mind if I'm hauling a suitcase."

"Fine," I said. "I'll carry your bag."

"And please do wear those pleated, grey-striped pants I like so much."

"Is that part of your fantasy, too?"

"Of course!"

"Very well."

And so I trundled off to LaSalle Street station in my pleated pants carrying Maurice's mint green suitcase. I watched him as he approached the ticket taker to explain that a friend of his was helping him with his luggage. Then we walked the platform along with a gaggle of other excited travelers, making our way to car 3201, in which Maurice had a ticket for Room 5.

I looked up at the windows of the rooms. "Which side is your room on?" I asked.

"Oh, my God!" Maurice shrieked. "I forgot about that. What if it's on the other side? If it's not facing the platform, my whole fantasy will be ruined!"

"If that's the case, maybe you can ask the passenger across the aisle to swap with you, at least until the train pulls out of the station."

"Oh, bother!" Maurice's mood was quickly

deflating. "You'd better board the train with me. I'm going to need help getting properly situated."

"What about me standing on the platform waving good-bye?"

"There'll be plenty of time for that. The train doesn't leave for another twenty minutes."

"OK, fine," I said.

And so we climbed into Car 3201, Maurice with his scarf and cigarette holder, me with his mint green suitcase. When we got to Room 5, we discovered it was on the platform side of the train.

Maurice smiled broadly. "Now, Elly, sit down. I want to explain to you how I want this next part to work."

"Fine," I said and I sat in the seat.

"Here's the way it is," Maurice began. "I'm a little bit worried about you, Elly. I can see how unhappy you are. And it has occurred to me that since I'm going off and leaving you, you'll end up sulking around my apartment without the benefit of me being there to keep you away from the razor blades in my bathroom."

"I'm not *that* bad, Maurice."

"Perhaps not. But nevertheless I've made other arrangements for you."

"What are you talking about?"

"Now, don't be mad at me, Elly, but I've gone out on a bit of a limb."

"What?"

"I telephoned your secretary, Peggy. She's very nice.

We got along very well. She had a lovely attitude about the whole thing!"

"A lovely attitude about what?"

"I spoke to Peggy and she agreed with me that it was high time you had a vacation."

"What are you talking about?"

"Peggy looked in your records, Elly. Did you know you haven't taken a vacation all year? It's the middle of October. What are you waiting for?"

"I'm not waiting for anything."

"Well, that's good. Because I arranged with Peggy to speak to your boss."

"You spoke to my boss!"

"No, not me. Peggy did. She spoke to Junior. I believe that's what she called him. And Junior agreed that it was as good a time as any for you to have your vacation. You're entitled to two weeks, but we only arranged for one. I hope you don't mind."

"You arranged what?"

"Well, surprise, I bought you a ticket. You're coming with me right now on the 20th Century Limited. We're going to New York! Together! You're just down the aisle in Room 9. Isn't that a pip?"

"Oh, Maurice!" I was shocked. I didn't know what to think. "But what if Vito telephones me while I'm gone? He's expecting me to be at your apartment."

"I thought of that," said Maurice. "I arranged to have Minnie stay at my apartment while we're gone. If Vito telephones, she'll let him know where you are and tell him that you'll be gone for a week. I gave her the telephone number of the hotel where we'll be staying. She'll call you to let you know that he's called. And she can give Vito the number if he wants to call you directly."

"Well, I guess that's OK."

"Come on. Cheer up! We're going to have a fabulous time. Isn't it exciting? Tomorrow we'll be in New York!"

"But Maurice, I didn't bring any luggage. What am I supposed to wear every day?"

"Ha. Ha! I tricked you there. You see, I've secretly arranged something else with Minnie. Minnie has surreptitiously transported your luggage to the train today. As a matter of fact, I looked from the platform before we boarded. She's already here! She's waiting in Room 9 with your luggage. You see it won't be you standing on the platform waving goodbye as the train pulls out. It will be Minnie. Isn't that marvelous?"

"Maurice, I don't know what to say."

"I hope you're not disappointed."

"No. It's just … well … I'm in shock. It's going to take me a few minutes to adjust to this idea."

Maurice looked at his watch. "Well, dear, the train is leaving in ten minutes. I suggest you go down to Room 9 and let Minnie know the cat is out of the bag. Otherwise, she'll be getting nervous about de-boarding before the train leaves."

I was stunned by what Maurice had done, but on

the whole I was thrilled. This was certainly an adventure that would distract me from my woes. I gave Maurice a hug, then began to make my way down the aisle to Room 9. As I walked, I wondered what clothes Maurice and Minnie had picked out for me to wear on this trip. I began to wonder what I was going to do in New York. I was in a complete state of wonderment when I arrived at the door of Room 9. The door was closed. I knew Minnie was waiting for me inside. I could have just walked in. But then I thought perhaps it would be polite to knock first. So I knocked.

32

I knocked on the door.

The door opened.

But Minnie was not inside.

"Hello, Elliot," Vito said.

"Oh, good God!" I screamed it loud enough for everyone in Car 3201 to hear me. "What are you doing here?"

"I'm going on a trip to New York."

"I don't understand. You're going to New York? Where's Minnie?"

"That's one of Maurice's little tricks. He's quite a playful fellow, Elliot. And I can now say from experience that he cares a great deal about you. Minnie isn't here. She was never going to be here. It was always going to be me. Nice pants, by the way." I was standing in the aisle. Now I stepped into the room and closed the door.

"What was always going to be you?" I asked. "I don't get it."

"Of course, you don't. It's a long story. The short version is that Maurice talked to Minnie. Minnie talked to Leonard Lehnert. And then Minnie talked to me. The original idea for this fantasy trip came from Maurice. But it was Minnie who came up with the added touch of keeping you in the dark until we got you onto the train."

"You planned this? All of you together?"

"Yes, Elliot. Maurice, Minnie, me, and, uh, Leonard Lehnert."

"I don't understand. What did he have to do with it?"

"The Lehnerts are paying for the trip, both for the train fare and for our hotel in New York. Believe me, I thought a lot about the ethics of that. But after thinking about what they did, why they did it, then what you did, and why you did it, I decided, hell, why not? Besides, it was the only way we could come up with the money for this on such short notice."

"So … I take it … you … you got my letter?"

"I did."

"And I take it, you've decided to give me another chance?"

"Elliot, it was wrong of me to tell you to leave. I'm sorry for what I put you through. It was wrong for you to read my letters. But you couldn't have known why that would upset me so much. I've had experiences that have made me especially touchy about what you did. When I was a boy, my father found a hidden scrapbook I'd made. I'd spent months secretly cutting out pictures from magazines. They were all pictures of men I thought were handsome. I even included a picture of four men from the Sears catalog in their underwear. My father didn't say a word. He took off his belt, told me to drop my pants, and whacked me with the belt until his arm gave out."

"Jesus."

"Then there was that incident, which I think you heard about through Minnie, in which the petty officer on my submarine went poking around in my sea bag and found Frederick's letters. I wasn't court-martialed, but it was humiliating. And when you poked around in the closet and found the letters, too, it put me right back in that same situation."

"Oh, Vito. I'm so sorry."

"I know." He looked deep into my eyes. "Elliot, your letter to me was beautiful. It made me feel more loved than I've ever felt before. I don't think you know how much that means to me. And I want to be able to help you feel as good about yourself and as loved as you've made me feel. I realized as soon as I read your letter that I wanted you back."

"You did?"

"Yes. But I didn't have any way to contact you. You didn't put anything in your letter about how to reach you. I knew Maurice only by name. I didn't know his telephone number or where he lived."

"What did you do?"

"I went to the Dome Room. It was Tuesday night. I'd just read your letter that afternoon. I knew from what you'd told me that Tuesday night was when Minnie performed and that Maurice was a regular there. So I figured it was a good place to start. But I waited too late. It was after ten o'clock. By the time I got there, Minnie's performances were over. I found out that I'd just missed seeing you, that you and Maurice had been there. Apparently you left just before I arrived."

"I can't believe it."

"Yeah. I was that close. But luckily I was able to get Maurice's telephone number."

"Did Minnie have it?"

"Uh, actually, it was Frederick who had it. Maurice had only just written it down for him before you left. It was a lucky break."

"So Freddy was still at the Dome Room when you got there?"

"Yes. And I must say, he was in a much better mood Tuesday night than when he was at that funeral. From what I could tell, his mood was due to Maurice. Frederick was completely smitten. It doesn't surprise me in a way. They have common interests."

"Maurice told me he thinks Freddy is a dreamboat."

"Well, I won't argue with that."

"But Vito, how did all this happen? I mean this trip to New York."

"Well, since it was so late, I decided to wait and telephone Maurice the next day, which was Wednesday. You were at work. So when I called, it was Maurice who answered. And he just came up with this whole scheme spontaneously. He said there was no point in having a reunion if we didn't do it in style. And I guess it was partly because he himself had just found out about his meeting with the New York producer. So he was about to go down to LaSalle Street station and buy his tickets."

"How did the Lehnerts get involved?"

"That was Minnie. After talking to me, Maurice called Freddy, who gave him Minnie's telephone number. Then Maurice called Minnie to get her advice about the scheme. It was Minnie's idea to have the Lehnerts pay for the cost of everything. She seemed to think they could easily afford it and that they owed you something. So Minnie talked to Leonard and he agreed to pay. Maurice is the one who made all the final arrangements. He booked these rooms on the train. He booked our hotel in New York. And then he arranged to have me bring your luggage here and surprise you."

"You brought my luggage?"

"Well, of course."

"So Minnie was never here?"

"No. Are you disappointed?"

"God, no! I'm just in a daze. But I ought to go back to Maurice's room and thank him for all this."

I turned around to do that, but Vito put his hand up to block me from opening the door. "Wait a minute. Maurice and I discussed this also."

"Discussed what?"

"Maurice knew you'd want to thank him. But he felt it would be better if you and I made up before you thanked him."

"Made up how?"

"I can think of a good way we can do it." Vito moved his body close to mine.

I looked around. "Can we do it in here? There's not too much room."

"There's an upper berth and a lower berth. Which one do you prefer?"

Just then the train whistle blew twice and the Pullman cars lurched forward. I fell into Vito's body. Once again I was cradled by his massive arms. If there was a point when I left Vito's arms during the next few hours, I just can't recall it. And yet, I remember everything.

ACKNOWLEDGMENTS

I'm grateful to Michael Priebe, who edited this novel. We spent many lovely hours together working on the manuscript. Michael gave me invaluable help with plot details in addition to editing and improving the text. Any errors remaining herein are mine alone.

I'd also like to thank Karl Koch for his outstanding cover designs for both books in this series.

I gained insights into what it was like for LGBT people during World War II in the military and in Chicago in 1948 from the following books:

• *Coming Out Under Fire: The History of Gay Men and Women in World War II* by Allan Bérubé

• *Chicago Whispers: A History of LGBT Chicago before Stonewall* by St Sukie de la Croix

I learned about the ins and outs of being in the Navy during World War II from the book *Sea Bag of Memories* by William J. Veigele.

My radio dramas were inspired by the online archives of the *Adventures of Philip Marlowe* starring Gerald Mohr. The episode called "The Persian Slippers" was the inspiration from which "The

Fortune-Teller" episode was derived. The episode called "The Hiding Place" was the inspiration from which "The Johnny and Vance" episode was derived.

Finally, thank you to Kale Williams, whose wonderful recording of *The Winkler Case* audiobook helped me hear Elliot's voice within *The Shadow's Voice*.

ALSO BY DAVID GREENE

The Winkler Case

The Winkler Case is Book One of the Elliot Blake novels. When insurance salesman Elliot Blake makes a house call at the home of fight promoter Walt Winkler, it's handsome boxer Vito Vellucci who comes to the door. In this gay re-imagining of the classic noir novel *Double Indemnity*, obsessive desire unfolds in an unexpected direction.

Unmentionables

Unmentionables is the epic story of two couples in the Civil War south. One couple is straight, white and wealthy; the other is gay, black and enslaved. Field hand Jimmy meets Cato, a house servant from a nearby plantation. Over time, Jimmy's fascination with Cato grows into romantic love. *Unmentionables* won the 2010 Book of the Year bronze medal for LGBT fiction.

All to Pieces

The epic gay Civil War saga continues in this second installment in the *Unmentionables* book series. Slave catchers kidnap Jimmy and resell him into slavery. Cato risks his own re-enslavement to travel deep into Confederate territory in an all-out search to find his lover.

Detonate

Ride from Niagara Falls to New York City on a speeding
train with biracial, bisexual private eye, Tyrone King, and
fellow passenger, Sarah, as they race to stop terrorists from
blowing up the Statue of Liberty.